*Everything and
Nothing*

Everything and Nothing

Nilotpal Kumar Dutta

tara
India Research Press

tara
India Research Press

Flat. 6, Khan Market, New Delhi - 110 003
Ph: 24694610; Fax : 24618637
www.indiaresearchpress.com
contact@indiaresearchpress.com

2019

Everything and Nothing
Copyright © 2019 Nilotpal Kumar Dutta

ISBN 13 : 978-81-8386-170-0

Printed and bound in India for Tara-India Research Press.

To my grandparents,
Durga Devi & Ugranarayan Dutt
Kamla Devi & Raghuvansh Kanth

PART I

Kandiya akul hoilam bhobonodir pare
Mon tore ke ba paar kore?
Mon tore ke ba paar kore?
Oshomoye ailam nodir pare…

I cried relentlessly on the bank of the eternal river
Who would sail you ashore o my soul?
Who would sail you ashore?
I came to the riverbank at an odd time…

Chapter 1

The old cuckoo clock on the wall chimed nine times. Zafar's gaze moved towards it, alternating between the dial and the swaying pendulum. Sitting at the window of Damyanti's bedroom, his wife, Rehana, and he were looking intently at the street outside. Every now and then, Zafar would go to the edge of the window, hold the rods firmly, and stretch his neck to look at the farthest point on the street. Not able to see things clearly, he would strain his ears for even a hint of a sound of a mob approaching or people crying.

Zafar and Rehana had been waiting impatiently for the 9 o'clock news on Doordarshan to assess the situation in riot-affected areas.

Three days ago, on December 6, 1992, a mob of *kar sevaks* driven by the Ram temple rhetoric had climbed the top of Babri Masjid and demolished it. Angry, agitated, and hurt, Muslims had come out in large numbers in various parts of the country to protest. More often than not, these demonstrations had resulted in clashes between the two communities and forced the police to intervene, causing damage to property and loss of lives. Most of northern India was simmering with tension, and the worst affected areas were Gujarat, Uttar Pradesh, Assam, and Bombay. However, amidst this turmoil, Patna had remained calm.

Both Zafar and Rehana dreaded this calm. To them it seemed like an indication of an ensuing storm, as if a high-intensity bomb could explode any moment and engulf the entire city. That hundreds of weapon-wielding men would break into Damyanti's house any second, drag the couple out, and kill them with knives and axes. So scared were they that in the large bedroom – which had a spacious sofa along the wall and a large king-size bed – they had perched themselves for hours in a corner on two small chairs. The corner, with strong walls on both sides and a clear line of sight to the main door, gave them a feeling of security, and the adjoining window a view to the deserted streets.

In those turbulent times, when trust was scarce, they knew they could only trust Damyanti when they took shelter at her's. Not only did they feel safer in her house, but also her presence itself gave them a sense of security. Most people in the neighbourhood, acquaintances, friends, and family would not have believed that the two were staying there. Not that there was any animosity between them, but the last few months had been very trying for Zafar,

Rehana, and Damyanti, often bringing them on the brink of cutting off ties that had otherwise always been full of love and affection.

So engrossed were Zafar and Rehana in listening to the news that they did not notice Damyanti enter the room.

At 82 years, the 5feet 6inch Damyanti exhibited immense confidence and calm. With long hair, mostly grey with a scatter of black strands that seemed to have faded with time and tribulation, sharp features, restless but tranquil eyes, fair complexion, and poise, Damyanti looked like an older version of the goddess she worshipped, whose portrait hung prominently on the walls of her bedroom and living room.

'Shall I ask Ramu to serve dinner?' Damyanti asked and then noticed that the plate of *pakoras* she had served the couple a few hours back was barely touched.

'No, *chachi*. We are not hungry,' Rehana answered softly.

Damyanti walked towards the couple, caressed Zafar's head, bent to kiss Rehana on hers, and whispered, 'Don't worry, I will not let anything happen to the two of you. I have spoken to…'

Her last few words drowned in the sound of the television. She turned towards the TV and began listening to the news. The anchor was describing incidents of communal clashes in various parts of the country, death of innocent lives, and damage to property. As she listened, tears rolled down her eyes. She wiped them gently, and, not being able to bear what she was hearing, slowly walked over to the adjoining room.

Lying on the bed, she stared at the ceiling fan. Unable to control her tears, she sobbed softly, 'Has *anything* changed in the last several decades? Have things not become worse?"

Lamenting what she had heard, her thoughts meandered to the decades gone by, tough and trying times, full of despair and loss. The fear that she saw in the eyes of Rehana and Zafar, the way they huddled in the corner, the look of hopelessness and impotent anger were not very different from what she had seen in her husband, Gautam's eyes, and he in hers when they had themselves hidden for a week to escape the bloodthirsty mob in Noakhali.

She had seen interviews and speeches of political leaders spewing venom and hatred not very different from what she had heard so often before the independence of India and over the last twenty years. As glimpses of decades past flashed in her mind and a wave of melancholy engulfed her, she whispered to herself, 'Nothing has changed and nothing will.'

With the winter-chill piercing through the thick blanket that she had wrapped around her body, several images crossed her mind. She reminisced her beautiful days in Dacca, her unwilling and tragic flight from the city that she loved and still did, the bloody mutilation of her large nation, the ill treatment of her people by the Pakistan Army, and a series of heart-breaking incidents in the times after.

All Damyanti had wanted was to live her life with her friends and family in Dacca. And here she was, alone, away from the city of her heart after losing almost everyone very early in her life.

Damyanti had never wanted to leave East Bengal — the place of her birth, childhood, and youth — in spite of her husband insisting that they move to Calcutta, the city of hope. How could she leave the house that she had built along with her husband; where her two sons were born and took their first steps; where she had sown every plant with her own hands and watered with ample love and care; where she had stood under harsh sun and, at times, heavy rain, supervising the laying of each brick; where every corner had a story to tell, stories that opened floodgates of memories? How could she live without the abundant love showered by her friend Samina, an affection that she treasured and still wanted more? How could she be away from the place, that had the comforting presence of Salim, Manas, and other friends; Salim, who most of the times appeared as a distant apparition, and on a few occasions still had a looming presence in her thoughts? How could she pull herself away from the grand *Durga Puja* celebrations at her father's house, a few rows away from her own? How could she not be a part of the city's *Janmashathami* procession?

She would have continued to live in Dacca had the Noakhali riots not happened. Noakhali was where her husband's family lived, and she had gone there along with him to visit her ailing mother-in-law.

On that fateful day of October 10, 1946, dressed in a white sari with thick red border, and a blood red *bindi* adorning her forehead, she was walking along with her husband, Gautam Roy, to her sister-in-law's house to attend *Kojagari Lakshmi Puja*. Still a kilometre away, Gautam saw the mob coming, wielding sticks, clubs, knives, axes, and many other dangerous weapons. It did not take him long to understand that the mob was of Muslim men in search of Hindu families. He held her hand and they ran like a pair of deer running away from hungry lions. Unsure of where to go or seek shelter, they knocked on the door of the house of Samina's aunt, who they barely knew. And, the old woman, in her late sixties, living all by herself with both sons away in Dacca, hid them in the servant quarter.

Holed up in that dingy servant room, praying that the rioters would not catch them, she had witnessed, along with her husband, one of the most horrifying of human massacres.

It was one week of living in fear and fright. And every time that they heard the maniacal sounds of the attackers and heart-rending wailing of the attacked, it was a near death experience. But even then she had argued with her husband that they should not leave East Bengal. She had blamed the Muslims of the western part of India for brain-washing the Muslims of East Bengal. She had argued that the Muslims of East Bengal, gullible in her opinion, would have never wanted the division of Bengal had they not been swayed by the wily Muslims of western India. She had argued that time would settle all the dust and things would go back to how they once were, like in the days of her child-hood, back to the Bengal that she had known and dreamt of. Like always, she figured that this time too she would prevail and persuade Gautam to abandon all thoughts of moving to Calcutta.

It was after a week in that servant room — not com-pletely aware of the enormity of the tragedy outside — that they had stepped out under police protection and into a refugee camp. In that single week, things had changed beyond recognition.

Gautam's younger sister had been raped, abducted, and murdered. His uncle's family was butchered in front of the eyes of its only surviving member, a young boy of seven. Gautam's other uncle had converted to Islam and was now known as Hanif and his wife, Sarita, as Gauhar. Half the locality that had survived had converted to Islam, and the other half was in refugee camps. It was told, and established through self-declaration, that the conversion to Islam was out of choice and not coercion. It was estimated that over

7,000 Hindus were killed; around 50,000 to 85,000 survivors had taken shelter in temporary relief camps in Comilla, Agartala, and other places; and around 50,000 Hindus that remained marooned were living under Muslim supervision.

Damyanti had become numb and almost lifeless as she began her life in the camp. That her Muslim brothers of East Bengal carried so much hatred to resort to such merciless butchery and destruction escaped her comprehension. The truth was that she had failed to realise the sheer extent of the divide created and still, whenever Gautam spoke about moving to Calcutta, remained quiet. Even after witnessing the mass killing and destruction by fellow Bengalis, she had blamed the outsiders, held them responsible for sowing the seeds of hatred and mistrust between Hindus and Muslims, and of the ugly propaganda declaring the Partition of Bengal, and India, as the only solution.

With a deep breath, Damyanti came back to the present. She took another deep breath and moved to the edge of the bed to see Rehana and Zafar. They seemed even more frightened than earlier, probably the effect of the news. She kept looking at them as they stared at the television. Several thoughts troubled her. Would Patna, her place of residence now, become like Noakhali? Was this really the calm before a storm, a disaster waiting to happen? Scared to live in the neighbourhood, would Rehana and Zafar move out of their home, as she had half a century ago?

Her thoughts went back to the refugee camp that she

had moved to after Noakhali. Having lost hope, she did not protest when Gautam had mentioned Calcutta again. They had left the camp, never to go back to East Bengal again. She had wanted to live in a place that would be immune to such hatred. Even while leaving, she had only prayed for the happiness and success of the people she was leaving behind. But her prayers were in vain; things had taken a darker turn. East Bengal, a part of Pakistan after the division of India, began receiving step treatment from its national government.

Every time she had read Samina's letters detailing the treatment meted to East Pakistan by Pakistan Government, her heart had gone out to the people who had been family to her. Samina's news on the deteriorating condition of Dacca and East Bengal made her cry. She had often prayed for the intervention of a saviour, someone who could fight for the people of East Bengal, who could get from Pakistan what was rightfully due to the Bengalis, and if possible free them from the clutches of the power blocks in West Pakistan.

Governments are supposed to work for their people, provide them security. The Pakistan Government had failed in its duty towards its Bengali citizens. And for the past few decades, various governments in her country, India, had also failed in their responsibility — often, deliberately, out of greed to meet personal and selfish electoral objectives.

With the liberation of East Pakistan, Damyanti had only envisaged happy days for both the nations that she considered her own, India and Bangladesh. She was confident that the two countries would learn from their harrowing experiences and all communities would live peacefully with mutual respect and love.

Sadly, though, almost half a century after India had gained independence with the loss of thousands of lives in communal clashes and twenty years after the bloody war of independence of East Bengal, nothing seemed to have changed. And, testimony to this were Rehana and Zafar, frightened and scared, hiding away from their own people to save their lives.

Damyanti had reminisced her entire life in a short time — a life reflective of India before and after independence. Everyone who knew her during her childhood, college days, in her professional environment, and later, always thought of Damyanti as a very strong woman. She had studied to be a doctor when very few women ventured to get formal, professional education in the British Empire. She had always exhibited confidence and knowledge beyond her age. She was the one many looked up to emulate. But in her heart, only she knew that she had failed so many times — sometimes for a lack of will to fight, and at times, because of a failed sense of judgement, not being able to read situations correctly. Her own people had suffered because of her, and she lived with that burden of guilt.

A tune played on the TV; the news was over. She got up, walked to Rehana and Zafar, and spoke in a soft, commanding tone, like Samina's aunt had all those years ago, 'You need to eat. Don't punish yourself. Everything is fine. Your *chachi* is still around.'

Chapter 2

Damyanti's deep attachment with Dacca was not only because of the wonderful times that she had had while growing up and after her marriage with Gautam, but also due to her family's long association with the city. The Ghosh family had considerable influence in Dacca and enjoyed tremendous goodwill of the people across all strata. Family members and friends would often share memories of how so many had benefited from the enterprise and charity of her great-grandfather and grandfather. As a child, these stories filled her with awe; and as a young adult, they left her with a sense of admiration and pride.

Equally deep-rooted was Damyanti's relationship with Samina; an association across generations, built on trust and shared values. Their two families had been acquainted for many decades, had stood by each other in times of need, and celebrated moments of happiness together. This was a subject of envy for many and of pride for the members of the two families.

Damyanti was born in 1911. A daughter after three sons in Nakul's house, her birth was a matter of great celebration for the family. Old grandfather Ghosh, overjoyed with the news, distributed sweets to one and all, and with each sweet that he personally handed over, he made it a point to mention that Goddess Lakshmi had arrived in his home.

Though from a prominent family, great-grandfather Sujoy Ranjan Ghosh, born in 1810, 6feet 2 inches tall, barrel chest with strong arms and legs that every wrestler in the area was scared to challenge, was not a man of letters, but one of infinite wisdom. He had come to Dacca to learn and engage in the lucrative trade of jute. As a young man, he travelled 300 kilometres from Rangpur, up north of East Bengal, to Dacca in the southeastern direction. The journey along Jamuna-Brahamputra for the most part and on land for some part was an example of courage and fearlessness. The Bengal jute industry had started emerging as a strong competitor to the Scottish jute industry, and he had understood that there was a fortune waiting to be made as a middleman between jute cultivators and the businessmen of East India Company, who exported shiploads of the fibre to Great Britain. And, he did make a fortune, one step at a time, with grit, determination, a lot of hard work, and a bit of cunning.

A keen observer, he saw gradual growth in the middle class from a society, primarily agrarian, that comprised of either rich or poor. The East India Company needed people to work and the numbers of the English were not enough. He did not possess enough knowledge to clearly understand what the future would look like, but the continuous activities of the East India Company and his interactions with their officers gave him a sense that the time to come would bring in big changes. And most importantly, he understood that the ability to communicate with the English, the aptitude to appreciate their ways and science would be a differentiating factor. He recognized the importance of adopting the western system of education and thinking, and advocated that everyone should do so. He would argue with his friends, urging them to send their kids to schools run by English-speaking teachers, emphasizing the importance of learning the language.

By the year 1857, Sujoy's eldest son was studying in Dacca College and the two younger sons in Dacca Collegiate School. His life revolved around his business and close-knit circle of friends that included Imran, Abhishek Talukdar, Davinder Dussanj, Pranesh, and Ashraf. Imran and Abhishek belonged to families of *Zamindars*. Davinder, a Sikh, owned a grocery business, and Ashraf was a farmer.

A decade earlier, Ashraf's younger brother, Karim, had joined the Bengal army of the East India Company against the wishes of his elder brother. The Company had divided India into three presidencies for administrative purposes, and each of these maintained its own army. Karim was a part of Bengal Native Infantry (BNI) regiment.

In the month of April that year, Karim came back home, unexpected and unannounced. His regiment had been disbanded. In March 1857, word had spread in the regiment that the new cartridges supplied to the soldiers were wrapped in papers greased with cow and pig fat. These needed to be opened by the mouth, thereby hurting the religious sensibilities of Hindu and Muslim soldiers. It resulted in an argument between the soldiers and the colonel and then an open revolt. The regiment was stripped of uniform and disbanded.

In the last week of April that year, worried that Karim was without work, Ashraf walked down to meet his friend Sujoy to request him to teach Karim the art of jute trade. Sujoy gladly accepted and took him on as a protégé. Karim's decision to work with Sujoy and learn the trade from him not only laid the foundation of one of the most established businesses in the city, but also of a relationship between the two families that stood the trial of times and always succeeded.

Karim was a native Bengali, and he took a lot of pride in it. His family had been Buddhists till a few centuries earlier and had converted willingly under the influence of Arab traders and Sufi saints unlike other parts of India that had witnessed conversions by force and coercion. One of Karim's forefathers had fallen sick as a boy, and the local *vaid*, not seeing any hope of recovery and survival, had pronounced his impending death. His mother had held him in her arms and had run several kilometres to a Sufi saint, promising to God that she would adopt Islam if her boy survived. The saint blessed the boy, touched his forehead, and poured a few drops of water from an earthen pot. Full of belief and devotion, the mother refused to leave the place of the saint. In three days, the boy was as healthy as ever, as if he had never fallen sick. Immediately after that, she argued with her family and talked them into adopting Islam.

The revolt of the soldiers of the BNI regiment resulted in a war of independence with the sepoy mutiny. Though the Indian soldiers had a few initial successes, they were defeated eventually. Karim was very sad. No one would have prayed for the defeat of the English more than the soldiers of the Bengal Native Infantry.

Sensing his disappointment, Sujoy, many years elder to Karim, put his arm around his shoulder and consoled him, 'Do not worry. The English will eventually be forced to leave India. The time has not come as yet. It may not come in our lifetimes, but it will. And till then, let us focus on our business. These are changing times, impacting the common people. Let us work hard to build a business that will give employment to many and will help in the overall development of Dacca. Let's work towards a Dacca and Bengal that our future generations will cherish, where they will live with peace and prosperity in complete harmony.'

'*Dada*, do you actually believe that someday we may be independent?' Karim asked.

'Yes, Karim. Perhaps not in our generation, but I'm sure one hundred years from now we will be a very powerful country, extending from Kashmir in the north to Kanyakumari and Nicobar in the south, and NEFA in the east to Baluchistan in the west. Our history, heritage, and combined struggle against the English will teach us to live together. We will have a government run by elected representatives who will be totally devoted to the betterment of people and the nation, like in England and America. After having experienced centuries of oppression, our leaders and people will work selflessly to ensure happiness of each other,' Sujoy paused, laughed, and spoke as if prophesying, 'I'm so happy for the life that our great grandchildren and their future generations will live. They will experience freedom and joy in Dacca. They will be a part of a large powerful nation. The country will have leaders who will be united, irrespective of religion, caste, or region. They will toil to keep the nation as one and work to take her to unimaginable heights.'

Sujoy's prophecy turned out both right and wrong. India became simultaneously independent but mutilated. The country did adopt a democratic form of governance, but with time the leaders became greedy and selfish with little interest of the public at heart. And, one person who was greatly affected by all this was Sujoy's great-grand-daughter, Damyanti. The dream that he saw for his grand-children was fulfilled in some ways but failed in many.

Sujoy died many decades before Damyanti was born. But his belief about 'One Bengal', a unified and strong India built on combined orchestrated resistance to the British, a modern India educated on the progress made in science, and a country ruled by its own people and not kings and monarchs, had passed to the young girl. The discussion that Sujoy had had with Karim that evening was in some form not different from the discussions that she had so often heard in her own house while growing up. Sitting on her grandfather's lap, she had often heard him speak to his friends the way Sujoy had that evening, and had felt confident that nothing could go wrong, that the times ahead were going to be happy and that she had nothing to worry or fear. The hope that emanated from Sujoy that day, the optimism for a bright future for India and Bengal was ingrained in her grandfather and had passed in the same measure to her. Cocooned in her own world, away from the complexities of the world and showered by love from all, Damyanti had no reason to believe otherwise as a child.

Sujoy and Karim had immersed themselves completely in the jute business. Karim leveraged on the experience and wisdom of his mentor, and their businesses grew and expanded to other areas. Sujoy took an instant liking to his younger partner, whom he found to be extremely honest, hardworking, sincere, and self-less. And, Karim never missed expressing his gratitude for the immense contribution Sujoy continued to have in building his business and career. If Karim managed to negotiate a better deal with the jute planters, he ensured that the advantages were also passed on to Sujoy. And, in cases where such benefits could only be passed to one of them, he would silently, without informing his mentor, divert such deals to him. Later, when Sujoy would come to know from other planters such acts of selflessness, he would chide Karim, but with affection and love. Sujoy relied on Karim's sense of judgement and respected his intuitive power and networking skills, which, much like his, was raw and earthy, but a tad more sophisticated. Many British officers looked at Karim with suspicion given his background at BNI, but Sujoy's intervention and assurance always helped tide over such situations.

And gradually, with time, the business relationship evolved into a deep bond between the two families. Sujoy's wife was like an elder sister to Karim's wife, whose opinion she always sought. And, Karim was the go to *kaka* for all children, always loving and caring. There was no festival or celebration at Sujoy's house where Karim's family was not actively involved. And on every Eid, Karim's children would first walk to Sujoy's house to get *Eidi*, and only after generous gifts from him would they go to their father. When Sujoy's youngest son, Dinanath, had fallen sick and no amount of treatment was helping in his recovery, Karim had travelled to Calcutta along with him and begged the British army doctor, who he had served with and had immense faith in, to treat the boy.

As a result, the relationship between the two families only grew stronger. They spent a lot of time with each other, celebrating happiness and standing by each other in tough times.

When the first railway lines were being laid in East Bengal between Dorshona in Chaudanga district and Jogtree of Kushtia district, Sujoy sent his youngest brother and eldest son to look for civil construction work and supply of labour to the English contractors. They made a lot of money working with the English officers. Unfortunately, in October 1865, exactly three years after the railway operation commenced, Sujoy's son died of a fatal snakebite at the young age of 27. The English doctor was not in station. The villagers tried all the medicines and tricks, but with no luck. They tried to extract the poison and applied local herbs. A woman engaged in black magic was called when herbs failed to work. Nothing could save the young man. His body turned blue and he died with foam coming out of his mouth.

Sujoy could not bear the loss of his eldest son and fell sick. He started growing weak with grief. His other sons were still studying. After a couple of years, he became bedridden from heavy pain in the left side of his body. A man of strong intuition, he knew he would not live long. He was worried that his business would collapse with his sons still in college. Not only did he need someone to take care of his business for a few years, but also look after his family. He called for Karim one evening — not his brother or any of his friends — and with tears in his eyes, requested him to take care of his business and family till his sons learnt to manage the trade. Karim cried seeing the state of his mentor, choking with emotion. He held his hand and promised him that he would treat the young kids as his own blood and would always give priority to Sujoy's business over his own. Sujoy passed away in his sleep that same night. His face looked composed and relaxed the next morning.

As promised, Karim lived his duty with the highest integrity and honesty. He remained a pillar of strength for the Ghosh family, always there for them in times of need and happiness. There was no Durga Puja where he did not supervise the arrangements, working out the finer details. The words of Sujoy's wife, his *Boudi*, were his command, and the Ghosh family took no decision of importance without consulting him. The business too flourished, and both Karim and Ghosh family made a lot of riches.

Chapter 3

Sujoy's youngest son, Dinanath, had been in college in Calcutta the night Sujoy passed away. It was decided that the elder brother would take complete responsibility of business, and Dinanath would continue with his studies and choose a profession of his liking. He had been a very bright student, the brightest in the outgoing batch of Dacca Collegiate School in his year. Sujoy would often tell everyone that his youngest son would become a barrister and he would spend whatever was required for his higher studies.

Now Bengal was changing rapidly. Bengalis, especially Hindus, adopted the English system of education in large numbers and many undertook higher studies. Several students went to Britain to study law and to prepare for Civil Services. Dinanath had also planned to go to England to study to become a barrister. Education was a great leveller. It gave Indian students confidence that they were as good as the English. Education created a new elite and a prosperous middle class. Sadly, the Bengali Muslims continued to remain aloof, away from the English system of education, barring a few exceptions. The new educated middle class and the wealthy landlords of Bengal felt that their aspirations could only be met by self-rule or a larger involvement in governance and policy making. Gradually, the desire to have a say and influence in governance led to the nationalist movement.

Dinanath's elder brother was very hard working and had a great relationship with the locals and jute growers. But he lacked the charm to interact with the English officers, charm that had all but defined Sujoy so well. Not being able to manage close relationship with the English officers, the business started declining. Even Karim was not of much help as the English officers looked at him with suspicion since he had been a part of Bengal Native Infantry.

While at home on a break from college, Dinanath sensed trouble in business and at home. He asked his mother and *Boudi* if anything was wrong, and when he did not receive a satisfactory reply from them, he walked up to Karim's office. After a lot of persuasion, Karim told him reluctantly, 'Our trade has taken a beating. We are not able to manage the English officers. They don't trust me much and your brother is struggling to develop a relationship with them.' Sounding sad and distressed, he continued, 'We have made commitments to the farmers and given some advance in anticipation of orders from the English merchants, but the orders don't seem to be coming. The farmers will not return the advance paid to them, and they will dump the jute on us, which may just go waste. We suffered a lot last year. We need orders before the season starts.'

Dinanath was listening patiently. He could sense worry and fear in Karim, and asked him, '*Kaka*, what is your suggestion for me?'

'Dina, come back to Dacca if you can and manage your business. Only you can help us build back our relationship with the English officers and merchants. Many families have become dependent on our business, and we have many commitments. This is your father's dream. He wanted to build the largest business house in Dacca and provide employment to hundreds in Bengal. Though he was keen that you pursue your interests and not join the business, if things continue as they are now your father's dream may meet its death,' Karim pleaded.

Dinanath met all the English officers and merchants over the next two weeks. They found him sophisticated, suave, and intelligent. In no time he had not only won their affection but also their respect. A few of them, who had interacted with Sujoy, found him to be a sophisticated version of his father.

Before leaving for Calcutta, he went to meet Karim and told him, '*Kaka*, I will not go to Great Britain or pursue any other profession. But please allow me to complete my studies before I join the business, and till then I will help part time.'

Karim hugged him and cried, not letting him go. Dinanath looked blank over Karim's shoulders, devoid of any emotion. His own dreams were nothing compared to the problem that both families had in front of them, the benefits and good that could come to Dacca. His father had dreamt of a prosperous, industrialized Bengal; a Dacca where many could earn their livelihood; and where his subsequent generations would not only live in harmony and happiness but also engage to make it greater than ever. How could he let that dream die?

It had not taken Dinanath more than a week to decide where his priorities should lie, but it took him years to overcome the pain of letting his dream go. The week to decision was torturous for him. He tried working out various alternatives by which his brother could manage the business without him, but he was ultimately convinced that none would work. The more he analysed the situation, the stronger his conviction grew that the business needed him; his father's dream required his active participation in the day-to-day affairs. He held back his tears during his stay in Dacca until he boarded the train for Calcutta. He cried through the journey and in the arms of his friends in his college hostel.

Dinanath's actions were deeply appreciated by his family and friends. Damyanti's grandmother would often tell her this story with pride, a story of sacrifice by her husband, a sacrifice not only for his immediate family but also for the larger good of the people of Dacca. What struck the young child most was that her grandfather had killed his dreams so that so many families in Dacca, both Hindu and Muslim, could continue to earn their livelihood. As a child, narration of such incidents, stories about the contribution made by her family strengthened her ties with Dacca further; it built a belief that if anyone had any claim on the city it was she, and if she ever needed any help there would be many families standing for her. There were so many who were touched by the charity and goodness of the Ghosh family; and it had not gone unnoticed by the young child.

Trade and business were not merely means of livelihood and earning in the Ghosh household. Very early in her childhood, Damyanti had learnt that the objective of business for the Ghosh family was also the betterment of the people of Dacca and the development of the city. As a child, she had often heard her grandfather ask whenever a new idea was shared, 'So how will this help our people of Dacca? How many people will get employment because of this?' Since her early childhood, she was cognizant of the deep attachment that the family had with Dacca, and it only bolstered her own relationship with her city of birth.

As industries flourished, Bengal witnessed a lot of development. Nowhere was development of Bengal more visible than in Calcutta, the British capital of India. Several Hindu landlords and businessmen from East Bengal moved to Calcutta.

As Calcutta developed, Dacca, the one-time capital of Bengal during the Mughal rule was left behind. Also, unlike the Mughal rule when landlords were mostly Muslim, a lot of Hindus became landlords in the colonial times. Adoption of education leading to various professional and government services made the Bengali Hindus economically stronger. With growing disparity in economic conditions and educational status between the Hindus and Muslims in Bengal, there was resentment building in Bengali Muslims, and nowhere was it felt more than East Bengal where Muslims were in majority, primarily earning their livelihood as peasants. This had not escaped the notice of the English. It had also not escaped the notice of Karim, old but still strong. Used to the ways of the English when he was in the army, he always suspected that they would use it to their advantage.

With time, the British Government became more oppressive, enacting laws and Acts that the educated Bengalis found discriminatory. Along with many eminent personalities of that time, Dinanath joined the Indian Nationalist Association and later the Indian National Congress when it was merged into it.

In the month of July, 1903, Karim's failing health deteriorated further. His breathing became heavy, the pain more acute, and body weaker. Battling heavy rain one evening, Karim's grandson came to Dinanath's house with the message that his condition had worsened and he wanted to meet Dinanath. Dinanath ran all the way to meet his *Kaka*.

'Dina, I may not live long,' Karim said in a feeble voice the moment he saw Dinanath, 'I am indebted to you for agreeing to join the business on my insistence, such a sacrifice of burying your own aspirations. I am also thankful to you for never making any distinction between your business and ours, and then forming a combined venture with the production mills. You have always been fair.'

'I learnt from you, *Kaka*. You have been like a father to us after the sad demise of *Baba*,' Dinanath said, sitting beside Karim, who was lying on the bed and holding his hand.

'And I learnt it from your father, Dina. What a fine gentleman, so selfless when it came to his friends, so devoted towards the betterment of Dacca and her people.'

Dinanath enquired about Karim's health, they chatted for some time, and then Karim spoke, placing his hand on Dinanath's hand, 'How is your work progressing with the Indian National Congress?'

'I have not been too involved with INC, *Kaka*. The mills have been taking a lot of time.'

'Dina, why don't you enrol more Muslim members in the Congress?'

Dinanath was taken aback with the question and could not understand the reason for it. 'But *Kaka*, the membership is open to people of all religions. Have you heard of any discrimination, or felt so?'

'There is growing discontent amongst Muslims here. Hindu landlords have moved to Calcutta and have invested in other businesses there. Lack of education in Muslims and relative poverty is creating a divide between the Hindus and them. Calcutta is in a position today that the Muslims here feel should have been that of Dacca. The community feels left out and neglected. And they fear that the situation will only become worse for them.'

'But *Kaka*…'

Karim interrupted Dinanath, 'I have worked with the English in the army. I understand them well. A section of the Congress has started asking for *Swaraj*, self-governance, threatening the basic existence of the English in India, and *Swadeshi*, locally manufactured goods, which will impact their factories in Great Britain and their economy.'

And then, lowering his voice, Karim continued, 'The English are portraying the Congress as a Hindu party as the leaders are largely Hindus. They have been asking Muslims to form a separate party. They will divide the Hindus and Muslims to quell these ideas of *Swaraj* and *Swadeshi*. And if there are two parties, with two different and divergent views, the English will continue to rule without any change in situation.'

'*Kaka*, I have heard about this, but I am sure our Muslim brothers of Bengal will never want another party.'

'Dina, we are Bengalis, you and I. But it will be *outsiders* who will cause disharmony. They were *outsiders* who came along with the Mughal army and started influencing our culture. If we get divided between two parties based on religion, it will not be because of Bengalis, but *outsiders*; the English and the Muslims from United Provinces, Punjab, and Sindh.'

'*Kaka*...'

A servant walked in with a large tray with plates filled with snacks and two large glasses of tea.

'Come closer, Dina,' Karim said, as he lifted himself to sit on the bed, reclining against the wall to have his tea. 'Do you remember Robert Burn? He was a very close friend of your father?'

'I had met him in my childhood. Hasn't he gone back to England?' Dinanath asked.

'Yes, he did. But his youngest son married a Muslim girl from a noble family and settled in Calcutta. He visits Dacca once a year and always meets me during his stay. He is close to the English officers in Calcutta, but is a sympathizer of Bengal.'

Dinanath was getting a hunch that he was going to hear something ominous. His body was stiff and ears completely focused on Karim *Kaka*.

Karim lowered his voice and spoke in a whisper, 'Burn tells me that the English are planning to divide Bengal into two administrative regions; the Muslim dominated East Bengal and Assam, and the Hindu majority West Bengal, which will be clubbed with Bihar and Orissa.'

Dinanath choked as he sipped tea, started coughing badly, and slumped in his chair. 'Bengal divided…' he muttered.

'*Outsiders*… not native Bengalis,' Karim said, as if apologetic about the impending division.

On October 16, 1905, Viceroy Curzon declared the division of Bengal. The Hindu majority, western Bengal was clubbed with Bihar and Orissa, and the eastern part of Bengal was clubbed with Assam for administrative purposes.

A few days later, Karim had severe chest pain but refused to see doctor. He called for Dinanath, held his hand, and cried like a baby. 'This division is not merely the division of Bengal but indicative of the gory times to come. It is quite possible that Muslims may found a party for themselves. Fight this, Dina, fight it hard. Please do not let the *outsiders* win. But if you see yourself losing this battle, please move to Calcutta.'

That same night, with his family around him, he breathed his last.

***

The division of Bengal saw lots of protests. Public at large, mostly Hindus and a few Muslims, started boycotting English products and institutions. There was a fierce cry for *Swadeshi*; boycotting English textiles, educational institutes, and several products. Calcutta became a hotbed of an already existing nationalist movement taking a more aggressive and assertive form.

But as protests increased and boycott of English goods took its toll on economy, the English announced reunification of Bengal in 1911. The division was now on linguistic basis for administrative reasons; Bengal and Assam as one region, and Hindi-speaking Bihar and Oriya-speaking Orissa clubbed as one Province.

The reunification of Bengal brought cheer to every Bengali household. There were festivities everywhere. Amidst this jubilation was born Damyanti. Whenever someone in the family spoke about the reunification of Bengal, inadvertently the discussion also moved to Damyanti's birth. To the young, impressionable child, Dacca appeared conjoined to her existence.

At her birth, Dinanath held his granddaughter in his arms, close to his heart, and told everyone with joy, 'My *Paki* has brought luck to Bengal. She is a princess and I will name her Damyanti. She will live like a queen in Dacca, a life filled with happiness and joy. And Dacca will always protect her like a mother.'

The saga of the division of Bengal and the eventual reunification was lived and discussed in each Bengali household not only for those six years but for many years after 1911. And, nowhere was this discussed more than the Ghosh household. As a child, Damyanti would often hear stories not only from her grandfather but almost all the elders of the family about the ill-intentioned division, strong resistance by common people, the selfish objective of the *outsiders* to divide the two communities, and the eventual defeat of these evil forces with reunification. The reunification brought a lot of hope to Dinanath. The six years were fraught with anxiety, but to him the reversal of the decision was indicative of people wanting to be together, that the common people would not let the cunning ways of the *outsiders* succeed. His belief in the idea of 'One Bengal' and one single nation in India only grew stronger. And gradually, unknowingly, through stories told, that hope rubbed off on his granddaughter.

He never stopped mentioning to Damyanti that her birth had brought luck to Bengal, and how all despair had ended the year that she was born. The struggle for reunification of Bengal was his favourite story to his granddaughter, and the eventual outcome in the blessed year that she was born a reason to cheer for the grandfather and granddaughter. Nothing was more music to her ears than her grandfather saying that it was she, her birth, which brought the divided Bengal together. To the young girl, such a statement coming from a person who was held in awe and respect by everyone left a deep impression in her mind.

When her grandfather told her that in spite of suggestions from most he never lost hope and the idea of leaving Dacca never occurred to him, Damyanti knew that should a similar situation arise in the future, all she needed to do was let her hope live and hold the fort. And when, in his deep voice, he said, 'Dacca will take care of you, Bengal will take care of you', she had no reason to think otherwise.

Coming from her grandfather, the thought gave her immense comfort, a feeling that can only be felt and understood by a child.

Chapter 4

By the time Damyanti was six, the Ghosh family, spread over Dacca, Calcutta, and other parts of India, had emerged as one of the most influential families in Dacca.

Mukul, very dear to Dinanath and the only son of his deceased eldest brother, had moved to Calcutta many years back to oversee the construction and operation of the mills. The number of mills had grown, and so had other trading businesses that he had set up under the family's flagship company. He was one of the earliest members of Calcutta Club, which was founded in 1907 when Indians were refused entry to the all whites Bengal Club. Though not in the forefront of the nationalist movement, Mukul was a member of the think tank and a strong financial donor. He had three children.

Dinanath's other brother, who had four children, had passed away a few years back. Both his sons were living in Dacca and were involved in the family business. His daughters were married into wealthy families, one living in Dacca and the other in Sylhet.

Dinanath had four sons. His eldest son was a barrister in Calcutta with two children, both boys. His second was working as a senior officer with the railways, posted in Allahabad; the third was married to an English woman and was involved in the family business in Dacca; and his youngest son, Nakul, was a doctor trained in England.

Nakul had returned to Dacca and set up his medical practice near the main market. He had four children; Damyanti was the youngest, born after three brothers.

Damyanti was a bright child, full of life, loved by one and all. She had the fearlessness and charm of her great-grandfather Sujoy, confidence and sophistication of her grandfather Dinanath, and the intellect of her father Nakul.

As a child of six, her world comprised of her family and six friends. Her friends lived close by, always eager to sneak out of their homes to play together. Though younger than everyone except Samina, who was the same age as her, Damyanti was the undisputed leader of her group. No game could start till she had announced her arrival and no result declared till it had her concurrence. Her friends loved indulging her. At an age when fights and hurt are natural and common, her wishes were always entertained and commands obeyed. And if there was ever a voice or a point against what she said, Salim would intervene and ensure that her wishes were complied.

Three years senior to Damyanti, Salim, the great-grandson of Karim, was the eldest of the group and the most intelligent. He could never bear to see Damyanti in pain, always careful not to hurt or let anyone hurt her. His affection for her had not gone unnoticed by the others in the group, including Damyanti. She enjoyed Salim's gentle care and would often even create situations for him to intervene on her behalf. She loved such moments when he stood up for her, even when she was in the wrong, basking in his attention. She knew when to approach him to get the prized place to hide in the game of hide and seek or choose a position of advantage in any other game, knowing full well that her requests would never be turned down. And, Salim was always eager to oblige, looking for opportunities to bring a smile on her face.

Apart from the brother and sister duo of Salim and Samina, the other members of the group were Arup, Tapan, Manas and Parineeta. Arup was Damyanti's elder brother, older by a year, calm and composed even at that young an age. Tapan was Abhishek's great-grandson, living a few houses away from Nakul's house. Manas, who was protective of his cousin Damyanti, was the son of Dinanath's third son. Parineeta was the daughter of Dinanath's nephew, son of his elder brother.

Damyanti was very happy in her world, busy with her friends and loved by her family. She knew that like her father, grandfather, and great-grandfather, she too would live and die in Dacca. She belonged to Dacca and, at that young age, felt that Dacca belonged to her.

She was eight years old when one day sitting next to Dinanath in the courtyard, she asked, '*Thakurda*, did you marry *Thakurma* to bring the two families together?'

Dinanath laughed, and asked, 'Who told you this, *Sona*?' Everyone addressed Damyanti as *Paki*, her pet name, but Dinanath called her *sona* out of love.

'Ma, *Thakurda*.' Damyanti replied innocently, as Dinanath continued to laugh.

'Yes, *sona*. My *Baba* and your *Thakurma's* uncle were very close friends. They wanted their friendship to be converted into a relationship. And, I was made the sacrificial goat.' He laughed louder. Dinanath was married to Abhishek's niece.

Dinanath was lying on a string cot, enjoying the sun, and Damyanti was sitting beside him, lost in thought.

'*Thakurda*, will you also get me married to someone to bring two families close?'

Dinanath laughed loudly, uncontrollably, and just said, '*Sona*, my *sona*.'

Not wanting to leave the topic, with hope in her eyes not noticed by her grandfather, she asked, '*Thakurda*, are Rehman *Kaka's* family and our family close to each other?' Rehman was Salim and Samina's father.

'Yes, *sona*.'

'Very close, *Thakurda*?'

At that moment, her father Nakul walked in to discuss something important with his father. They got involved in a discussion and Damyanti, after waiting for some time and realising that the conversation would take time, walked into the house, dejected.

Growing up, she would often hear her aunts and grandaunts talk of how they wanted their sons and daughters to live close to them. Hearing them yearn, she would pray to God, requesting that their wishes come true. And then, she would see her aunts and cousins get married and move away from Dacca amidst tears that would refuse to stop. She also saw her uncles and cousins moving to Calcutta for higher studies and settling there or in other cities because of jobs.

As the years passed, she began to realize that many things in life were beyond one's control. She wanted to live with her friends in Dacca till she grew old. They were all precious to her, some more than the rest but would time separate them?

'Why would anyone want to leave Dacca, my beautiful Dacca,' she often wondered. 'Will I have to leave Dacca because of my marriage? Will Samina and Parineeta leave as well to live with their husbands? Will Salim, Arup, Manas, and Tapan go to Calcutta for studies and then settle there?' These thoughts continued to trouble her.

One day, while playing, she asked, 'Samina, when you grow up, what will you want to do?'

Without applying much thought, Samina replied, 'Be a wife. Take care of my home.'

'In Dacca?'

'Of course, Paki. Dacca is so beautiful. And I want to live with all of you.'

By this time the rest of the group had joined the two.

'Samina, I have an idea,' Damyanti spoke without losing breath, and continued, 'You marry my brother Arup and I will marry Salim. Tapan may marry Parineeta. With this, not only will our families come closer, but we will also continue to live together as friends in Dacca.'

'No. Not me. You marry whomever you want, but I will never marry Parineeta. She only fights with me.' Everyone immediately turned towards Tapan hearing his protest, failing to notice Salim blush.

While Damyanti was planning the future of her friends, the British government was planning to pass two Acts that year, impacting the future of Indian citizens.

The Government of India Act, 1919, was passed as Montagu-Chelmsford Reforms. Montagu was the Secretary of State for India and Chelmsford was the Viceroy. The Act, an Act of Parliament of the United Kingdom, was passed for greater participation of Indians in governance by establishing a dual form of governance in major provinces, a diarchy. In each of these provinces, nation building subjects of the 'transferred' list like agriculture, education, and public works were placed under ministers responsible to the legislature; and subjects in the 'reserved' list like finance, revenue, home affairs were looked after by nominated executive councillors.

In the same year, Rowlatt Act was passed, extending the emergency period of the First World War and authorizing the English government to imprison anyone on suspicion of terrorism for a period of two years.

Combined, the two Acts sent mixed signals to the public.

Though Bengal was reunited, the fissures in the two communities remained and each wanted greater political control.

One evening, the Ghosh family had gathered for a wedding. Looking at Damyanti decked in a kid's *sari* and jewellery, one of her aunts remarked, 'Next year, we will get Paki married. Paki, who will you marry?'

'Salim,' Damyanti immediately said.

'But he is a Muslim.'

'So?' Damyanti sounded puzzled.

'What will your kids be, Hindu or Muslim?'

'Hindu. They will be my kids, so they will be Hindus.'

Everyone laughed, except Damyanti's mother. Damyanti could sense a strong feeling of discomfort in her mother's eyes, an expression that stayed with her, and never went away completely.

It had not escaped Damyanti's mind that there was a subtle tension between members of the two communities. She was happy that this tension had not touched the families of Rehman and Dinanath. But her aunt's reaction and mother's cold stare belied her belief. All of a sudden, she felt her family was also not completely untouched by this feeling of discrimination, at least not her aunts and other women.

She began noticing Salim and Samina more closely, trying to find out the differences between them and her, their way of life and hers, simple things like the words they used while talking and the ones she did. The more she tried; to her happiness, she discovered more commonalities than differences.

***

The 1919 Act increased a flurry of meetings between members of each community, both trying to work out plans to have higher representation in the proposed elected provincial body. Though Dinanath was out of active politics and the nationalist movement because of failing health, he had people visiting every day to seek advice and suggestions. On many such occasions, Damyanti would, either discreetly or by accident, listen to conversation between her grandfather and the visitors.

She could sense a tone of urgency in their voices, a tone that seemed to indicate that they needed to act immediately else someone would usurp something that was precious to them. Standing behind the door left a little ajar, peeping in, she could see clenched fists and hear thumping on the table. And in raised voices, she could hear words like, 'Muslim', 'Our Bengal', and 'Our Rights'. She often heard the sentences; 'we cannot let our future be dictated by Muslims'; 'they had supported the division of Bengal'; and, 'we need to ensure higher representation in the provincial councils'.

In these high decibel emotion-filled meetings, she found her grandfather's voice to be the only voice of moderation, one that seldom lost control, and had a calming influence on all. More importantly, it had a calming influence on her. Hearing her grandfather speak in such meetings bolstered her belief that things may not be as bad as what others might make it out to be.

Though she was not able to understand the reason behind the rift between the two communities, the division was more visible to her now. Her own analysis had always indicated that there were hardly any differences. Hence, it puzzled her that if she as a child could understand this, why were older men and women unable to.

'*Thakurda*, is someone stealing away our house and property?' Damyanti asked her grandfather when the visitors had left, restless after hearing the conversation for many days.

'No, *sona*.'

'Then why does everyone talk about protecting our rights, properties, and other things?'

Dinanath pinched his granddaughter's cheek, 'My naughty *sona*. So, have you been listening to our conversations?'

Sheepish, but unfazed, she asked, '*Thakurda*, doesn't Bengal belong to both Hindus and Muslims?'

'Of course, it does, *sona*.'

'Then, are Muslims bad, *Thakurda*?'

Dinanath hugged his granddaughter, and taking her in his arms asked, 'Are your friends Salim and Samina bad?'

'No, *Thakurda*. They are very good. I love Samina more than Parineeta.'

'*Sona*, both Hindus and Muslims are not bad. All of us are Bengalis, with Bengal's interest in our hearts. We are like a family, we need to live together. We need to work together for the betterment of our people. And if we are together, no force can harm or divide us.'

'Which is this force trying to divide us, *Thakurda*?'

'Outsiders, *sona*, outsiders.'

'And who are these *outsiders, Thakurda*?'

Knowing well that his granddaughter might not understand, he still went on to explain, 'Well, for one, the English are *outsiders* to Bengal and India, *sona*. What is good for them may not be good for us. Also, Muslims, who are not Bengalis and have come here from outside or are staying in other parts of India, forget that there is a common thread that ties all Hindus and Muslims who have been a native of this land. They find the Bengali way of living of native Muslims as non-Islamic. Such Muslims are *outsiders* to Bengal, and I doubt the interest of Bengal and her people is in their hearts.'

Damyanti was listening intently, trying to fathom what her grandfather was saying. She could not understand completely, but understood that there were a lot of Muslims who were like her, Bengali, and their views and outlook were no different. She also understood that there were some *outsiders*, and that they were not good. The conversation with her grandfather and those that she had been overhearing made her realize that religions build a dividing line.

A couple of years later, one afternoon when she was back from school she saw a large crowd in her courtyard shouting and sloganeering in anger and engaging in scuffle with the guards and servants of the house. Passion seemed to be overtaking reason. As she walked by, she could overhear the crowd demanding that Bijoy, Nakul's compounder and assistant, be handed over to them. She saw Bijoy in a room with her father and grandfather.

'Do you want to marry her?' she heard Dinanath ask Bijoy.

'Yes, I do.'

'Do you realize that she is a Muslim, the daughter of a tailor known to many Muslim leaders?' Nakul was shouting.

Dinanath, weak and frail, wanted to say something, but was interrupted by his son, 'No, *Baba*. Let me speak to him.'

'Do you see the crowd outside, baying for your blood, trying to break in to get their hands on you?'

'I will run away with her.' Bijoy said meekly.

'Do you think they will let your family live in peace? Will your family let their family live in peace? Don't you realize how vitiated the atmosphere has become, people looking for reasons to make political gains, to create fissures between the two communities that already has so many cracks?' Nakul sounded worried and irritated.

He continued, 'The only future that this has is of darkness and blood, not only of your family but many other members of the community. My heart goes out to both of you, but…'

The sentence and the ones after that were drowned in the high pitch shouting and sloganeering.

She saw her father coming out without Bijoy. He spoke to the people outside as they shouted and argued. Nakul would often place his hand on the shoulder of the person he was speaking to, trying to calm him down. He spoke to all of them till it seemed that the anger had subsided. Gradually, the crowd left the courtyard.

Within a month of this incident, the girl was married to a Muslim boy. On her way back from the wedding, walking along with her father, she wanted to ask him if Bijoy could not marry the girl because he was a Hindu and she a Muslim. Her young mind knew such a question from a girl to her father would never be appreciated. But what was the point in asking a question the answer to which she already knew.

This incident and several other incidents left a deep impression on Damyanti's mind. She realized there was an apparent divide between the two communities, and, though it appeared thin, it was unbridgeable. She had expected her father to support Bijoy. But he did not help Bijoy and felt it would only be right that he did not marry the Muslim girl. Her mother had expressed her displeasure at the thought of her marrying a Muslim. She understood then that though Salim and Samina were Bengalis like her, they were perceived to be different. At a time when most girls were married by the age of 12 and 13, Damyanti finally understood that a marriage between Arup and Samina, or Salim and her would be against established norms and not possible.

The ten-year-old child in her did not know how to handle such situations. She would be angry without knowing who to be angry at and frustrated without anyone to express her feelings to. She was old enough to see, but too young to reason it out.

The following evening she did not approach Salim for any help during a game of hide-and-seek. She acted as if she had not heard him offer her the prized hiding spot behind the large drums. And when Tapan cheated her in the game of marbles, she didn't complain to him either. Salim noticed the change in her behaviour, went to her a couple of times, and then, lost in thought, went back home.

But Damyanti's behaviour did not change the next day and the days after that. All his effort to try and understand this sudden aloofness failed, leaving him hurt and confused. Salim refused to come out to play, preferring to stay indoors with books. But every evening, when Samina came home, he walked up to her to check if Damyanti was fine.

As the friends moved into their teens, they stopped playing together, spending less and less time with each other. The boys started spending time together, leaving the girls to form their own group. Over a period of time, Damyanti and Samina became closer, the bond stronger. They were soul sisters, sharing every dream and desire.

Meanwhile, the Nationalist Movement, the seed of which was sown in Bengal and nurtured by the early Bengali nationalists, had spread all over India. Mohandas Karamchand Gandhi returned to India in 1915 after running a successful campaign against the British in South Africa. He toured across India, meeting peasants, farmers, labourers, and common people, educating them against the oppressive tax system of the British and the immediate need for complete independence.

On April 6, 1930, Gandhi marched from his ashram in Sabarmati to Dandi to protest against the severe tax on salt. Though symbolic, the march helped rally common men as tax on salt impacted everyone. The Civil Disobedience Movement against the government was launched — English schools and colleges boycotted, English goods burnt, strikes all around. And on January 26, 1930, *Purna Swaraj*, Complete Independence, was declared.

On December 29 that year, Sir Muhammad Iqbal delivered an address in the All India Muslim League session propagating an idea of a single state, amalgamating Punjab, North Western Frontier Province, Sindh, and Baluchistan; a Muslim majority state — a separate Muslim-dominated country in the north-western part of India — Pakistan. Bengal was still not a part of this plan, which was in its nascent stage.

The year 1930 was also eventful for Damyanti and her friends. Salim, who was studying in Calcutta, left for England for higher studies. Rehman wanted Samina to get married before Salim left for England. She was married to Iqbal, a young and dashing Army officer employed with the Indian Army. In 1918, the King's Commission was opened for Indians and ten seats were reserved for them in the Royal Military College, Sandhurst. Iqbal was one of the early graduates of RMC, Sandhurst.

Seeing Samina married, Sita Devi, Damyanti's mother, wanted her daughter to be married also.

'And why won't you marry now?' Sita Devi was surprised at her daughter's refusal. 'We have marriage proposals of an ICS officer, son of a friend of your father, and a doctor, a distant cousin of Tapan.'

'I want to study.'

'And do what?'

'I want to be a doctor.'

'Like your father? No, you should marry and live a good life with such great marriage proposals coming your way.'

'Yes, I want to be a doctor like *Baba*, and like Kadambini Ganguly. I will practice with *Baba*.'

Kadambini Ganguly and Chandramukhi Basu were the first two female graduates in India and the entire English Empire, graduating in the year 1882. In fact, Kadambini was the first physician trained in western medicine in South Asia, finishing her medicine in 1886.

Sita Devi saw fierce determination in her daughter's eyes, a will to succeed and chart her own course.

'Practice with *Baba*? Your marriage, now or later, may take you outside of Dacca.'

'No. I am not going anywhere. I will live in Dacca, and only Dacca.'

'So, are you planning to go to Calcutta for your studies?'

'Yes, I will try for an admission in Calcutta Medical College.'

Sita Devi was lost in thoughts while Damyanti sat like a statue anticipating a bitter argument between the two. 'I will ask your *Baba* to write to Mukul *da* so that you can stay with them. I will also ask him to write to Arup, requesting him to come and take you to Calcutta.'

Damyanti could not believe her ears. Stunned, she sprung up, ran to her mother and hugged her. Mother and daughter, both crying, remained in each other's arms for some time.

In a few months, Damyanti was on her way to Calcutta. Mukul had made all the arrangements for an admission in Calcutta Medical College. A bright student, she did not face any problems in qualifying for the admission.

1930 was also the year in which Dinanath breathed his last. His body was carried in a large procession on the streets of Dacca, befitting his stature. People from all walks of life, nationalist leaders, businessmen, prominent members of society, and common men came in large numbers to pay their last respects to the man who had stood tall and fair, with the interest of Bengal and Dacca at the core of his heart.

Chapter 5

Though she loved Calcutta, Damyanti yearned for Dacca. She could hardly wait to complete her medical education, go back, and practice there. Her close circle in Calcutta comprised Tapan; Arup; Mukul's youngest son, Biswanath; and Rohini, her classmate from Calcutta Medical College. Soon, she was also introduced to Tapan's friend, Gautam.

Gautam and Tapan were staying in Eden Hindu Hostel, established in 1886 for Hindu students of Presidency College. Presidency College was called Hindu College when it was established in 1817 by Raja Ram Mohan Roy — Maharaja of Burdwan, David Hare, and others — and was renamed Presidency College, College of Bengal Presidency, in 1855, and brought under the University of Calcutta in 1857.

Gautam often accompanied Tapan when the latter came to meet Damyanti. Dressed in *khadi*, he would sit below a tree reading a book while Tapan spent time with his friend. He would wait patiently for Tapan to finish, and then the two would leave.

Seeing Gautam wait patiently every time, Damyanti could not resist asking one day, 'Tapan, your friend comes with you, and as a routine sits below a tree reading his book, waiting for you to finish your meeting with me. Doesn't he feel bad about being left alone?'

Tapan laughed and said, 'No, Paki. He is a bit of a loner and doesn't mind waiting. We usually have things to do, either go to the library or attend a rally afterwards. He comes along because your hostel falls in our way and this way we can go together.'

What Tapan did not add was that his friend's background was humbler than theirs and that Gautam was fiercely conscious of the difference between them.

Next time, when Tapan was leaving after meeting her, she walked up to Gautam to say a brief hello. And, in a few weeks, hello became a sentence, and before she realized, sentences became conversations.

Gautam found Damyanti very intelligent and surprisingly humble. Aware of her privileged background, he had expected her to be arrogant.

'Paki, let me treat you to fish fingers and coffee at India Coffee House. Come, join us,' Tapan requested Damyanti one day.

Gautam stood not too far from them.

'May I ask the occasion and reason for this benevolence?'

'Gautam has stood third in the entire university in BA.'

'Congratulations, Gautam. But then should it not be Gautam who treats us?' Damyanti said loud enough for Gautam to hear.

'Thanks,' is all that Gautam could manage to say.

'If you want Gautam to treat, you will have to satisfy yourself with just coffee. If you want fish fingers as well, please allow me the privilege,' Tapan laughed loudly, alternating his gaze between the two.

'I can treat you to fish fingers as well,' Gautam said in a feeble tone, looking at the ground but loud enough for the two to hear.

Several guests waved at Gautam and Tapan as they entered the coffee house. India Coffee House on College Street had emerged as a place for intellectual discussions and always had a large presence of members of the Communist Party.

'It appears that the two of you frequent this place,' Damyanti said, occupying a chair.

'Yes, we join our seniors here. Most of them are members of the Communist Party,' Tapan replied.

India Coffee House was a haunt for MN Roy, the founder of the Communist Party of India.

'So, are you members of the Communist Party?'

'No. But we relate to Marx and his views on socialism, the need for a certain kind of policy for the labour class. We identify with the Congress party too, as we believe it can be the only unifying force for a mass struggle for independence. I realize that the Communist Party will not have the strength to fight for political causes, *Purna Swaraj* being the ultimate goal. The party is in a nascent stage and the English are completely opposed to Communism. Tapan and I have been a part of several movements of the Congress, and in discussions with the Communists without being a part of either party. In fact, I worked very closely with Congress during the civil disobedience movement.'

Damyanti could feel the passion and sincerity in Gautam, and was happy to know that Tapan's friend had a voice.

'Is your wearing *khadi* a result of the Civil Disobedience Movement?' Damyanti asked with a chuckle.

'Yes, and also because I find it comfortable,' he replied with the same seriousness as earlier.

Moving the discussion to academics, Damyanti asked, 'So, are you planning to go to London for higher studies?'

'I am planning to do M.A. in Economics from Calcutta University. I cannot see myself going to Britain for higher studies. It will be against what I have so vehemently stood for during the Civil Disobedience Movement. I do not want to join the Indian Civil Services, or be a barrister. I want to teach. We have been able to oppose the English because we have a large educated class who is able to differentiate between right and wrong and act on it. I do not know by when we will be able to achieve *Purna Swaraj*, but whether we are an independent nation or continue to be under the British, our success as a nation will depend on how pervasive education is across cities and villages. The country will only be as good as the next generation. I want to be a professor, preferably in Calcutta, engaged in imparting education and values to the coming generation.'

Over the next few weeks, Damyanti found Gautam to be very genuine and his opinions very honest. The visits to India Coffee House became increasingly frequent, and with time Damyanti started looking forward to the visits. Gautam's family was originally from Noakhali, but his father had moved to Dacca and was working as a postal clerk. Determined that his son got the best possible education, he had always gone beyond his means to support him.

The discussions in India Coffee House centred on topics ranging from the nationalist movement to books and cinema. Damyanti observed that Gautam had a clear opinion on most topics, never biased; and if he did not have information, he was all ears, asking incisive questions. His knowledge was as impressive as was his willingness to learn.

On her request, he started helping her nephew, Mukul's grandson, with his studies. On Saturday evenings, he would walk up to the Girls' Hostel, and seeing him from a distance, the watchman would quickly send the maid to inform her. She would be ready by this time, waiting for him. She would immediately step out and the two would walk side by side to the College Street Tram Station. Gradually, with time, the tram journey from College Street to Esplanade, where Mukul's family lived, helped in bringing the two closer. Sitting next to each other, lost in sweet nothings, the two would be completely oblivious to passengers and stations. But for the conductor, who took upon himself the responsibility of informing the couple that the tram was approaching Esplanade, they would have always missed the stop. From Esplanade, they would take a rickshaw to Mukul's house. He would return to Eden after the tuition and she stayed the night. She would be back to her hostel the next morning and to India Coffee House in the evening. Tapan and Gautam would already be there, engaged in debate with their Communist friends.

This became a routine. Damyanti and Gautam looked forward to it. His presence had a very calming effect on her. Her views matched his. The more time she spent with him, her affection only grew stronger.

While Damyanti and Gautam were getting closer, the two communities were growing apart. The murmur for two different nations based on religion had started in college campuses too. Often, one would see small gatherings of students in the areas near College Street engaged in heated discussion about the division of India along religious lines.

One day, on their way back from India Coffee House, the friends saw a young man addressing a small gathering of students, mostly Muslims. The young man could be heard from a distance, his speech vitriolic, spreading doubt and fear in his audience as he spoke about a separate nation for Muslims. And the audience, young and educated, seemed to be agreeing with his every sentence, nodding vehemently, occasionally raising an arm with clenched fist amidst high decibel slogans.

'Salman!' Gautam uttered, identifying the man.

'Do you know him?' Damyanti asked.

'Yes, he is the nephew of Pir Shahzada of Noakahli. His family lives in the same village as mine. In fact, Pir *sahab* was very close to us, but I hardly know Salman.'

'I've seen him with students from the United Provinces. I didn't know he's from Bengal. I've hardly seen him with Bengali students,' Tapan said.

'Pir *sahab* was a true Bengali, a native Bengali, and an Ashraf. I have heard from my father that he always espoused the idea of Bengalis living together, Hindus and Muslims. He led a strong movement for reunification when Bengal was divided in 1905. He withstood the atrocities of the English forces, unwavering in his resolve as he led the protests. I am sure it would have pained Pir *sahab* to see his nephew propagate this idea. I find it hard to believe that this is Salman's view. A member of Pir *sahab's* family can never think about division on the lines of religion, dividing people who have only lived together and have not known any other way of living,' Gautam spoke in a voice that grew continually softer, 'I am sure he is saying this because of these *outsiders* who don't understand and appreciate our deep bonding, history, and connection over centuries.'

'*Outsiders!*' It sounded so familiar to Damyanti, having heard that very term from her grandfather on so many occasions. She had always dismissed demands for a separate state along religious lines as political rhetoric, often attributing it to the compulsions of electoral politics. She had immense faith that if it ever came to the division of Bengal and India, common people would not let it happen just like they had in the first decade of the twentieth century. So strong was her faith in the bond that people shared, a lot of it built around what she had observed between the extended families of her great grandfather and Karim, that she would strongly reprimand Gautam and Tapan, calling their anxiety unnecessary and misplaced.

By 1935-1936, members of the Muslim League had increased their demand for a separate nation. Though the Congress had members of both communities, it was mostly perceived as a Hindu party. The ongoing rift with the League only strengthened that perception. While the clamour was more for a separate nation in the northern part of India, Damyanti feared it might not be too distant in time when the demand for the division of Bengal would also start.

The discussion for division spread, and with time, Salman developed a large number of followers. The number of people eager to hear him talk about a separate country for Muslims had started to attract large crowds. Initially dismissive about the danger ahead and attributing it to misplaced enthusiasm of an individual influenced by Muslims of western part of India, Damyanti was jolted when she overheard Tapan's younger brother's friend, Farhan, one day.

'Why is Salman wrong? Even I am convinced we will live peacefully as two different nations, each pursuing its own growth and agenda.'

Damyanti could not believe this was Farhan. She stopped, turned, walked up to him, and rebuked, 'Farhan, do you realise what you just said? Are you saying religion is more important than the nation, than our Bengal, the Bengal that we have always seen as one?'

'I don't mean the way you have understood, *didi*. But as minority, we will never get full rights. We will be suppressed in a nation dominated by Hindus.'

'Are you aware how many castes and sub-castes there are among the Hindus, and how bitterly they are divided in various parts of the country? Why don't we look at dividing the country into multiple pieces and let each have their own piece?' Damyanti was irritated.

The two argued for a long time, each unwilling to see the point of view of the other. This was not the Farhan she had known. Farhan was very close to Tapan's younger brother, a part of the family, and supremely intelligent. The two men had practically lived together while growing up. If someone as educated and exposed to multiple cultures as Farhan could be swayed by the venom being spread, how could she blame people who were less privileged, less educated, less exposed to the intricacies of various cultures?

But this was not Farhan speaking, not the proud Bengali that she had known. This was his fear speaking, a fear inculcated over a period by poisonous propaganda. A propaganda started by Muslims who were not native Bengalis.

'May these *outsiders* be cursed,' she said to herself.

The visits to India Coffee House had brought Damyanti close to members of the Communist Party. In 1936, All India Students Federation (AISF), the students' wing of Communist Party of India, was founded. Although Gautam had begun teaching in the university by this time, while continuing his doctoral research, Damyanti and he joined AISF as one of its early members. AISF had members of all communities, with many Hindu and Muslim members, a big reason for them being drawn to the party.

Fearing that the Muslim League, largely dominated by Muslims of the western part of India who were gradually influencing innocent young men like Salman, would start demanding Bengal as a separate nation for Muslims, united or divided, Damyanti and Gautam formed a small group which began working towards building an opinion against the division of Bengal. The group held occasional meetings to demonstrate communal harmony and bonding between members of both communities. They held discussions on Bengali literature and culture, with both communities participating in large numbers, to indicate that being Bengali was above the religion they followed.

Damyanti could see the difference she was able to make through the group she had formed along with Gautam. They were able to influence several students, who began to campaign for 'One Bengal', an 'Undivided India'. And, many of these were Muslims. If she worked hard, campaigned widely, met more people, she could build a larger consensus. College campuses were breeding ground for nationalist leaders, and most agreed that she could make a big difference.

It was during this time of active campaigning that Gautam fell sick. He had high fever when he dropped Damyanti to her hostel in the evening. He was coughing heavily. They had planned a students' meeting the next day to demonstrate harmony between Muslims and Hindus and solidarity with the newly formed peasant wing of the Communist Party. Though Damyanti asked him to take rest, he came the next day to support Damyanti. His fever became worse, and when he did not come to India Coffee House the next evening, Damyanti was worried the most. She insisted that he get admitted to Calcutta Medical College Hospital, but Gautam refused, choosing to remain in the confines of his room. The temperature increased to 103 degrees, refusing to come down. Tapan washed his head multiple times, but to no avail. A doctor came to see him, gave some medicines, but there was no visible change, the temperature remained the same. On the third day, refusing to listen to him, Damyanti and Tapan got him admitted to Calcutta Medical College Hospital. His temperature remained unchanged at 103 degrees. Damyanti remained beside him in the hospital ward, refusing to leave his side. No one knew when she slept or took rest. Several doctors came and saw him, and not able to diagnose the problem, started giving up hopes of recovery. With little hope left, she went to the Kalighat temple to pray for his life. Prayers being her only recourse, she sat in front of the idol of Goddess Kali, lost in prayers for more than an hour.

Having seen her pray with tears in her eyes, an old priest walked up to her.

'*Maa*, why are you so worried?' the priest asked with concern. He looked into her eyes, and, before she could answer, said, 'Go back, *maa*. Maa Kali has heard your prayers. Everything will be fine.'

Damyanti got up and left. As she walked a few hundred metres, she came across a Muslim *pir,* looking for alms. Damyanti gave him two *annas.* The *pir* took that with a smile, looked at her, and said, 'You are worried. Why? Your worries are over, *beti.* Things will be fine.'

It had been seven days since Gautam had fallen sick. Damyanti rushed to the hospital and met Tapan outside.

'Paki, where have you been?'

Fearing the worst, she asked, 'Why? Is everything fine?'

'Gautam's temperature has come down. The doctor has given him barley to eat. He is feeling very weak, but is able to manage a few words. He has been asking for you. Go and meet him.'

Holding the pillar next to her, she slumped on the ground and stayed there. If Gautam had succumbed to the illness, she would not have been able to bear the loss. She got up holding the pillar, straightened her *sari,* and ran towards the ward.

Rohini had informed Gautam that Damyanti had been to the Kalighat temple.

Damyanti sat on the floor beside Gautam's bed, held his hand firmly, and started crying. She cried with her head on the edge of the bed, tears refusing to stop. Gautam was looking at her, barely able to utter her name. Tapan, standing close, gradually took steps backwards and moved out of the ward, leaving the two alone.

Damyanti sat like that for an hour. Gautam drew some strength and put his hand on her head, stroking it gently. He was fine in two weeks.

In a week from then, sitting in India Coffee House, Gautam asked her, 'Will you marry me?'

'Yes, in a few months, as soon as I finish my medicine course.'

They were married that same year in Dacca.

Chapter 6

'Oh my God! We have been getting one bad news after another. Why is this happening, Gautam? Ma Kali, please be kind,' Damyanti exclaimed, holding the letter she had received from her cousin Biswanath.

'What's the matter, Daam?" Gautam asked, taking his eyes off the newspaper he was reading.

'Biswanath says that there is still no news of Tapan, and Arup continues to be in jail. What is happening, Gautam? I met Samina yesterday. She has been so anxious about Iqbal's safety. I pray daily for his safe return from the war. We will go to Calcutta and visit Kalighat temple once all this is over.'

Biswanath's letter had reached Damyanti in the second month of 1943. Gautam and she had moved to Dacca a few years back. He had joined the University of Dacca as a professor of Economics. She was working as a doctor in the Government Hospital, not too far from their house, which happened to be in the lane next to that of her parents, who had passed away by then.

The young couple had built a beautiful house, completely designed to Damyanti's dream. The small lawn had several rows of plants, each selected by her and planted by the gardener under her supervision. In between the rows of flower plants was neatly laid grass, as if a green carpet concealed the patch of land. The backyard had a small kitchen garden and a tube-well in the corner. Damyanti personally watered all the plants and weeded each blade of grass that lost its colour. She loved sitting in the veranda and watching her two sons play in the grass.

She had always dreamt of living in Dacca. When she was a student in Calcutta, she awaited the end of her education so that she could return to her city. She had jumped with joy when she had received the news of Gautam's job at the university. But not everything had gone as she had wanted them to. She had wanted a life with her friends, those she had grown up with, her close-knit circle. She had always dreamt of sharing small joys with them on endless rounds of tea and chatter, sitting in the familiar and relaxed environment that only Dacca could offer. The only friend who had remained in Dacca was Samina. With time, Damyanti had realized that it would be foolish to expect everyone to live there, but then Dacca was like a mother to whom her children kept coming back. She looked forward to their visits, eagerly, till she started losing hope. 'These ungrateful children', she would think. 'Maybe helpless.' She missed Tapan, Arup, Parineeta, Manas. And, most of all, she missed Salim.

She wanted Salim to see what she had achieved. Had he ever thought that she would train to be a doctor? Did he think that like every other girl she would get married early and be a housewife? She wanted him to see her consult patients, the confidence she exuded, and the respect she had earned. *Did she in some corner of her heart want to be a doctor to raise herself in his esteem? Silly thoughts*, she would dismiss. She wanted him to witness how Iqbal in his full military uniform, with a bit of seriousness and a lot of jest, often raised a toast saying, 'To one of the very few women doctors in the entire British empire.' She wanted him to feel proud of what she had achieved. But he had seldom been in Dacca; and even when he visited, he remained elusive.

Was he actually busy? Or was he trying to…

God had been kind to her in the last three odd years. And then, one after the other, the news started to pour.

First, it was about Iqbal, or the lack of it. Samina's husband had been sent to join the war for Britain in Malaysia, and there had not been any news from him. Then, it was Tapan. He was on the run after being released from prison, and there were no updates about his whereabouts. Lastly, it was about her brother Arup. He had been arrested and not been released for the last several months.

***

Tapan had joined the Indian National Congress around the same time Damyanti and Gautam joined the Communist Party. Nationalist to the core, and a very proud Bengali, he had heard people speak about the strong opposition of the Congress to the division of Bengal in 1905. He became an active member of the Congress, working against the divisive ways of the English and Muslims of western India, especially against the idea of a divided India and Bengal.

Two days before Christmas of 1935, Salman and his friends had planned a procession in various parts of the city demanding a separate nation. His procession was supposed to go through Park Street, which was decorated like a bride, and then congregate at the playground nearby. The procession was supposed to be a demonstration of intent and strength. Aware of this, Tapan and his friends had planned a parallel procession, congregating in the same ground. They had planned to sit silently in large numbers, Hindus and Muslims, against the idea of division.

The two processions marched to the ground from different directions amidst high pitch slogans. Salman's group, larger in number, was shouting for a separate nation. Tapan's group, with clenched fists and raised arms, was shouting *Vande Matram*. Salman was in the middle of his speech when Tapan's group came inside the ground and sat silently in the rear. The atmosphere was charged. Police was stationed outside to control disturbances.

'Muslims will never be safe in a nation with Hindu majority. Each and every Muslim wants a separate nation. And we will fight with our lives to take it.'

This was the fifth time Salman had mentioned this in his speech. Mudassar, an old tailor sitting behind Tapan, could not hold himself back, '*Beta*, I am a Muslim too. I do not want the division. We have lived together peacefully all these years. We are stronger together. Maybe the English wants us divided and weak so that they can continue to rule over us?'

Five Muslim youths, again a part of Tapan's group, shouted, 'We are Muslims too. We don't want this division.'

Amidst slogans from both sides, someone shouted 'traitor', picked up a stone, and threw it at the five youngsters. There was another stone thrown, then many more. Soon, Tapan's group started throwing stones at Salman's. Tapan was desperately trying to stop everyone, asking them to remain peaceful. Superintendent Wilson's men rushed into the ground and resorted to lathicharge, primarily on the men in the rear. Tapan and some of his friends were arrested and taken to Alipore Jail. Not a single person from Salman's group was arrested.

In jail, the police pressurized Tapan, asking him to confess that the protests were under the guidance of the Hindu Mahasabha. The British wanted to give the whole incident a communal colour, intending to profit from discord between the two communities. Tapan withstood torture for two weeks, until one afternoon when he was called by Superintendent Wilson himself and released.

It was Farhan who had gone to Damyanti, informing her about Tapan's arrest. When Damyanti failed to contact Tapan, she went to her uncle Mukul, the powerful businessman.

Two things happened after this. Superintendent Wilson's men felt Tapan had connections with powerful people, so every time he was arrested, which was often, he was released without torture. And, when Farhan rushed to Damyanti seeking her support to get Tapan released, her hope that Muslims would gradually be disillusioned with Salman and people like him, and live united, only became stronger.

However, unfortunately to Damyanti's dismay the cry and demand for a separate country for Muslims only grew stronger, with many more Muslims joining the movement.

In the winter of 1936-37, provincial elections were held as per the Government of India Act of 1935. For Damyanti, this was also a referendum on the division of the country, albeit in a small way. She prayed for the election of Congress governments in all provinces. More importantly, she wanted the Muslim League to lose, so that it became obvious that the people who wanted division were in a minority. Though she was a member of AISF, she canvassed strongly for the Congress, hopeful that a strong Congress would keep the country intact and not allow ill intentions of Muslim League to fructify.

The Indian National Congress won 707 seats out of a total of 1585 seats. Among the 864 assigned general constituencies, the Congress contested 739 and won 617. Muslim League won 106 seats, emerging as the second largest party. The Congress was able to form government in eight of the eleven provinces, the other three being Punjab, Sindh and Bengal. Though it emerged as the largest party in Bengal, the Congress failed to get majority, and was not able to form government.

No one was more devastated than Damyanti.

***

With Biswanath's letter still in her hand, sitting on a long reclining chair in the veranda with her legs straight, Damyanti was gazing at the narrow lane ahead, lost in her thoughts. The narrow lane appeared as a vast expanse of nothing as she looked ahead, unmindful of people moving. Some of them waved at her and some simply smiled. She reciprocated with a wave or a smile without making much effort to find out the identity of the person. The setting sun and the accompanying dusk had a soothing effect on her and she let her mind meander between the past and present.

How much had things changed for her and all her friends.

Parineeta was married into a wealthy landlord family with interests in agriculture and trading. A mother of four, she was happily settled in domesticity, lording over a vast retinue of servants. Her house in Sylhet was an envy of many.

Manas, after completing his graduation, had joined the family business and divided his time between Dacca and Calcutta. He was married and had kept himself away from politics. He would make it a point to meet Damyanti whenever in Dacca, showering his cousin and nephews with expensive gifts.

Her dear friend Samina was a mother of three. Samina seemed to be in a situation of constant conflict. While most people around her had immersed themselves in the nationalist movement, her husband was a serving officer in the British army. As a soldier and officer, his job was to protect the interests of the British government and fight her enemies. *Enemies!* Who could be enemies to the English? Wouldn't that be her own people? Such thoughts troubled her, and often she would express her dilemma to her friend and sister, Damyanti. Life had been good to her, her husband loved her, and she had all the possible comforts in her life. But the money and comfort appeared tainted to her.

Tapan and Arup were actively engaged in the nationalist movement. Tapan was single and Arup married with a daughter. While Tapan remained a strong activist, Arup more militant.

Salim came back from England and had remained single, immersing himself completely in his work. He could have chosen to work in his family business, but instead started a school in Dacca for the poor. He was also involved in the farmers' movement and various other welfare initiatives. He would always say, 'Sooner or later, India will become independent. We may not have enough educated people to manage the country when the English pull out. We need more people with proper education, a higher literacy rate among all strata. In fact, we need to remove gaps in society and make things more equitable.'

An acquaintance, A K Fazlul Haq, the Tiger of Bengal, kept requesting him to join the Krishak Praja Party. Salim, however, happy with the work he was doing, kept himself away from legislative politics. In his view, there was always time for that later.

Damyanti's own life had been fairly satisfactory. Did she not imagine a life like that of her mother and aunts, the kind of life Parineeta and Samina were leading? But here she was, a doctor, loved and trusted by many. She had been an early member of the Communist Party, but domesticity had kept her away from politics. She had a husband who loved her and stood by her like a rock. She had two beautiful boys, and she was sure that they would grow up to be intelligent men. Life had been smooth for her, and there was no reason why it would not continue like that. With a smile on her face, as she looked ahead, the narrow lane appeared unending.

The sun had set and her servants were putting lanterns outside. She stretched herself further as her memories went back to the days of childhood. The house in which she was living did not exist then. The house next door was also not there. There were trees and bushes in that area. She remembered hiding with Salim behind a tree in a game of hide-and-seek one evening, how he had revealed himself and hid her when Tapan came looking. She remembered her tantrums over boys playing marbles, forcing them to leave the area for the girls to play kit-kit. She could feel the love of her friends, a feeling that was still pure and devoid of any malice.

Her eyes closed and she went into slumber, lying there for a couple of hours. In her sleep, she saw a large procession, people being chased by men in red. The speed of the men fleeing increased, but so did that of the men in red. And then, only one man was left being chased by five. The man was coming towards her, asking her for help, outpacing the five behind him. She was able to see the face of the man only when he was close enough — her brother Arup.

She heard a gunshot, another one, and then one more. She saw Arup slump to the ground, without a word, lying in a pool of blood, his pride intact on his face. She turned on the chair with a slight start, but still asleep.

After some time, she saw a large fire. Thousands of people trapped, scared, and holding on to each other. There was fire all around, killing people and ravaging property. And then she saw Gautam and herself trapped in that fire, helpless, holding each other beside an idol of Ma Durga.

Amidst this mayhem, she saw her grandfather standing some distance from where she stood trapped with Gautam. He was calm, the only person unfazed in the chaos around, like he had always been. He was dressed in a white *dhoti* and a spotless white *kurta*. 'Don't worry, Paki, Dacca will protect you, Bengal will protect you,' he said. She looked around and found no one coming to help. 'Where are they, *Thakurda*?' she screamed, still confident someone would come. She saw an old man speak, old, but straight and strong. The man radiated strength, power, and had a unique aura around him. His *dhoti* was spotless, but *kurta* soiled and crumpled, as if he had waded through a large mass of people, fighting hard. 'Bengal is our land, Paki. We are one, tied across generations and centuries. Your brothers and sisters will protect you.' She looked at the old man in bewilderment and turned to her grandfather. 'Who is he, *Thakurda*?' Her *Thakurda* laughed his usual deep laughter, 'Your great-grandfather, Paki.' Assured that no harm could come to them, she released Gautam's hand and ran to her grandfather. He hugged her, caressed her head, and whispered repeatedly in her ears, '*Sona*, do not worry.'

Gautam came to the veranda and saw his wife in deep sleep. Not wanting to disturb her, he lifted her and took her into the bedroom. As he was gently placing her on the bed, she woke up with a start, remembering the two incidents. She shifted her gaze from the high ceiling to Gautam's smiling face and the strong walls of her bedroom. She felt his strong arms around her, felt safe and reassured, and realized that those two incidents were only dreams. Tired and drained, she just smiled at Gautam. She closed her eyes, felt Gautam's kiss on her forehead, and went back to sleep, a deep sleep.

In the months that followed, rarely did Damyanti have such a sound sleep.

Samina's anxiety had been growing by the day. There had been no news of her husband for more than a year. Iqbal was part of the Indian troop that fought the Japanese when they invaded Malaya on 8th December, 1941, at Kota Bahru, Kelantan. That same night the Japanese bombed Pearl Harbour.

The British army failed to stop the aggressive Japanese one, which continued to march ahead. Samina had heard that Iqbal was also there in the Battle of Muar, fought from 14th to 22nd January, 1942. The battle saw loss of three-fourth of the Indian Army, and by the time the Allied forces surrendered on 16th February, 1942, around fifty thousand had been either killed or captured. Even the retreat to the strong confines of Singapore did not help much.

Was Iqbal dead, had he succumbed to enemy fire? Or was he captured and holed in a prison, tortured by the treacherous Japanese? Did he survive the war and hide in some unknown place away from the Japanese forces? Or was he injured, lying immobile at the mercy of the locals? Did he lose a limb fighting the enemy? Or did the bullets just lead to wounds that healed with time? Such questions and thoughts troubled Samina frequently, and she felt that her head would explode. Troubled and shaken, she often rushed to her friend Paki, irrespective of the time of the day. Whether Damyanti was in the hospital or at home, never bothered her. No one could comfort her the way she could. No one's words gave her so much solace.

Whenever Samina heard news of the death of any Indian fighting in Malaya or Burma, she came to Damyanti, weeping. 'Paki, I hope Iqbal has not died fighting too,' she would wail. And then there were days when she locked herself in her room for hours, and when she refused to open the door after continued requests from everyone in family, it took Damyanti to come and plead her to come out.

'Gautam, I am very worried for Samina. She will kill herself with worry. I have been praying to Goddess Kali for Iqbal's safe return.'

'He will, Daam. The Japanese have occupied Burma, and they will advance to throw the English government here. If Iqbal is a prisoner of war, the Japanese need to be defeated for his release. They are growing stronger.'

'So, will the Japanese throw the English government and rule us, Gautam?' And then, Damyanti sighed and spoke again, loud and with pain, 'Again, a foreign ruler? *Outsiders?*'

Gautam squeezed her hand as he looked ahead in a blind stare.

The US Army bombed Hiroshima and Nagasaki on August 6 and 9, 1945. The Japanese surrendered on 15th August, 1945, and formally signed on September 2. The prisoners of war of the Allied Forces were gradually released.

Iqbal returned home on 13th October, 1945. He looked tired and old, so did Samina, having burnt herself out with worry. Iqbal had been made to work at construction sites laying railroads as a prisoner of war. Hard work, inhuman conditions, mental torture, and poor nourishment had taken toll on him.

Samina rushed to inform Damyanti about Iqbal's return. She ran like a woman possessed. The two held each other and cried with joy. A feeling of relief, hope, and happiness engulfed the two.

But the joy was short lived for Damyanti.

Fighting along with the Japanese forces were soldiers of the Indian National Army (INA), led by Netaji Subhash Chandra Bose. By November 1945, around 16,000 captured soldiers of the INA were brought back as prisoners of war. Many were interrogated and a few tried. As the soldiers returned home, post interrogation and release, they came back with horrifying details of the war and news of death of loved ones. One such soldier, Asif, brought the sad news of Arup's death. Arup, who had initially joined the INA to manage logistics, had moved to Rangoon. When the INA lost many soldiers, he trained to fight the British army. Asif had heroic stories to share of his Arup *da*, who had very little skill but unmatched courage. He fought bravely, till he became victim of a trap laid by the wily English.

Arup's wife fainted on hearing the news of her husband's death. Damyanti, busy consoling her sister-in-law and playing the role of a doctor to her, could hardly mourn the death of her brother.

That night, locked in her room, away from everyone's eyes, Damyanti cried inconsolably. 'Arup's family did not deserve this,' she kept saying to herself, holding her head close to her bent knee as she sat on the floor of her bedroom. There had been no news of Tapan and there was an eerie feeling within her that all was not well with him.

No one had heard from Tapan for over a year. There had been many rumours about his whereabouts, but no concrete information. Sibaram, whose elder brother was in INA, claimed he had heard that Tapan had followed Arup and joined INA. Manab, a doctor, told Damyanti he had overheard his patients talk about Tapan having died, succumbing to bullets in Imphal. Mukul, Damyanti's uncle, had heard that Tapan was killed by Muslim men, who saw him as roadblock to their idea of a separate country. A group, which had gone to Varanasi, claimed they had seen Tapan with sages who had come from the Himalayas. And some said that disillusioned with the building animosity between the two communities in Calcutta, Tapan went to Japan, married a woman there, and decided never to return.

Damyanti never heard from Tapan again.

'May these *outsiders* be cursed. May the English and people trying to divide the nation be cursed,' she shouted in the confines of her room.

The death of Arup and no news of Tapan was driving Damyanti into a state of depression. Every time she went to her ancestral home, she came back crying. The surrounding areas reminded her of the abundant joy of playing with friends. She would lock herself in her room and cry with a pillow pressed against her mouth, lest people heard her.

Her world was scattered; friends gone; and those surviving, doing it in pain. She lived in constant fear, but still hopeful that things would turn for the good. And amongst all this, the only constant was 'Dacca'. Dacca was like a mother, in whose lap she still felt safe.

'Daam, you need a change of environment. Also, there has been news that Bengal may either get divided or not be a part of India. We have lost,' Gautam said one evening, taking his spot beside Damyanti.

She remained silent.

'I have received a letter from Bhartiya Vidya Bhavan, Bombay. They will be starting a college shortly and have invited me to join as a professor. They have offered a good salary with an accommodation. Daam, we need a change of environment. A place outside of Bengal may be good for us in these uncertain times.'

Damyanti sat still.

A few weeks later, Gautam brought this up again.

'Daam, they have written to me again. I feel we should move to Bombay. So many people have moved there. I am worried about the division and unsure which side will Dacca be. We can always return after a few years, depending on the situation here. It will be good for our sons too,' Gautam was making an earnest plea, kneeling in front of Damyanti, holding her hand as she sat like a statue on a chair.

Damyanti got up. She looked at Gautam with a cold stare and spoke in a tone devoid of emotions, 'I will not go anywhere. I will live and die in Dacca. And Bengal will always be a part of India.'

The months after that were tumultuous, far away from what Damyanti and many like her had prayed and wished for.

Chapter 7

The end of the Second World War saw several beginnings. Though Great Britain emerged victorious in the war, her economic and military strength was reduced. The war saw the rise of two new global powers, the USA and USSR, and both supported India's demand for freedom. The Indian army, navy, and air force began to rebel in pockets, and the British army did not have the morale or energy to engage in a battle. The civil service and police, two vehicles used for governing India and suppressing freedom movements, were no longer as obedient to the English as earlier. On several occasions, the postal and railways staff went on strike. Governance and administration became a pain.

The end of the war also saw a change in government in Great Britain. The elections of 1945 saw the defeat of Conservatives under Winston Churchill and the shift of power to the Labour Party led by Clement Attlee. The Labour Party won the election with an agenda for reforms, and Attlee was more supportive of independence for India than Churchill was. In February 1946, Attlee declared in the House of Commons that a Cabinet Mission would be sent to India to facilitate the transfer of power.

In India, elections to the Constituent Assembly were held in July 1946. The Congress party won with two-thirds majority. The Muslim leaders feared that they would be voted out of the Constituent Assembly. They also feared that power might get transferred to the Hindus when the English moved out of India. The leaders of the Muslim League refused to cooperate with the Congress.

The League spread this fear to the common men in no time. The demand for a separate nation for Muslims grew stronger. Maybe, if left to the common people, both religions would have lived together peacefully. But the leaders of both communities had little trust in each other.

'Is it the lack of trust in the other community or is it the leaders' selfish desire and greed for power? These small groups of cunning leaders…' Damyanti wondered whenever she read about such incidents. The two communities often erupted into violence leading to riots, bloodshed, and loss of lives. Over time, the situation became worse.

'Daam, Bengal is like a matchbox, one small spark and it will burn down. We owe it to our kids to give them a safe environment to grow. Let us move out of Dacca. We have an opportunity today. The same may not be available tomorrow when we may need it.'

Damyanti was as adamant as earlier, not willing to leave Dacca, and so Gautam wrote back to Bhavan's College rejecting the offer. But as the demand for a separate nation grew stronger and incidents of riots increased, Gautam started fearing that the country might truly get divided or states reassigned on the basis of religious majority. Once again, he raised the topic of moving out of Dacca. As he had already sent a note rejecting the offer of the college in Bombay, he went back to his request of moving to Calcutta. 'If Bengal is divided, and not completely given away, Calcutta will definitely be in India', he would occasionally reason with himself.

'Daam, let's move to Calcutta. The way the agitation for a separate nation for Muslims has grown, I am not sure if India will remain as one country. And if the division happens, Calcutta has a higher chance of remaining in India.'

'Gautam, I am sure the common people of Bengal will reject the idea of partition. Didn't the partition of Bengal in 1905 fail?'

'Don't you see the numerous riots? Daam, the common people have not learnt anything from the partition of 1905, but the political leaders have. They will do anything to be in power. And they will not repeat the mistakes that led to the reunification of Bengal. They will fan fear in common people and make it appear that living in a Hindu majority country may not be in their interest.'

'Gautam, I don't know about other parts of India — Punjab, Gujarat, or Hyderabad. The Muslims there may want a separate country. But here, we are tied together with a single culture for centuries. We are Bengalis as much as Hindu or Muslim. I am confident we will never let religion come between us. Bengalis will never allow the division of their land on the basis of religion. Please be patient, Gautam. Things will be fine with time.'

Her voice became soft as she continued, 'You know, Gautam, the evil plans of these *outsiders*, their motive to split us on the basis of religion will be understood by my naïve Muslim brothers and sisters one day not far from now. We will remain one country.'

'Daam, you don't understand...' Gautam sounded desperate.

Damyanti interrupted. 'No, Gautam. I belong to Dacca and Dacca is a part of me. I have always dreamt of living here. Every brick in this house has my love embedded in it. Give the common people a chance, and you will see.'

Feeling drained, Gautam said a faint okay to Damyanti with a smile that refused to go beyond his lips.

A month from then, Gautam received a letter from his uncle staying at Noakhali. Gautam's mother was not keeping well. Fearing that she might not live long, Gautam and Damyanti left for Noakhali. Gautam's mother had become frail. In spite of her poor health, she dragged herself every morning to the market, bargained for the freshest *illish* fish, and cooked it herself for her son, refusing any help.

The ghastly riots started a few weeks into their stay. What they initially thought to be another procession turned out to be a mob of axe and knife wielding, blood-thirsty men. Damyanti and Gautam took shelter in Samina's aunt's house. The old woman hid them in the servant quarter that had remained unoccupied for months. The situation grew worse with every passing day.

Damyanti felt scared as the days passed — scared for her life and that of her family members; scared of the thought of her sons being raised as orphans; and most importantly, scared of the line that she now considered impossible to avoid being drawn, either through Bengal or along its border.

She wanted to run out of that room, run away from the mayhem. She even thought of running away from Bengal. She remembered her grandfather, his assurance that Bengal would always remain as one and that Bengalis are Bengalis first, people of the same origin and culture, and only then Muslims or Hindus. How she wished he were there to comfort her and prevent this catastrophe from happening.

***

"Gautam, you need to be brave. I have not stepped out of the house in the last seven days, but I have heard a lot. There has been a lot of...' Samina's aunt's voice trailed.

'Yes, *kakima*. Thank you so much for all that you have done for us.' Gautam touched her feet, and the two moved out of the house in hurry.

The street wore a deserted look. There was an eerie silence after days of mayhem. And, the silence appeared ominous. The doors of houses were either wide open or completely shut. Gautam was sure several houses were looted and many a death.

Around a kilometre away lived Sarita *pisi*, Gautam's aunt. 'Daam, let's spend ten minutes at *pisi's* house. We will check if they are okay and then go home.'

The door to the house was wide open. Gautam and Damyanti walked in and called for their aunt, but there was no response. They walked from one room to the other, shouting names of family members, but not a single voice came in response. Worried, they rushed to the backyard. And there, along the walls and on the floor, they saw bloodstains. There were haphazard lines of blood on the floor and walls, as if people had been dragged. They became conscious to a pervasive stench, of dead bodies.

Damyanti threw up. They rushed out of the courtyard, back into the house, and noticed bloodstains in various parts of the house.

'Daam, I hope *ma* is safe,' Gautam shouted in panic, held her hand, and ran like a man possessed. Panting, they entered the house. Gautam's mother was lying on a cot, just as he had seen her last. And sitting on the floor were his uncle, aunt, and a few more villagers.

'Where is Radha?' Damyanti asked as she looked around.

The world had indeed changed.

Radha had been abducted, raped, and murdered. Several families were butchered, including that of Gautam's uncle. Fearing death and retaliation, his other uncle and family had converted to Islam, and so had thousands of families.

Damyanti was numb, too shocked to speak. Gradually, a large group of people started gathering near the house; appearing shaken, tired, and lost. People sat on the ground, holding their hand, crying and wailing.

After some time, a group of officers arrived, asking people to move to a refugee camp. No one had the strength to argue. Gautam and his family could have gone to Dacca, but scared that something untoward might happen on the way and too dazed to think logically, they went along with the group to a temporary refugee camp.

Gautam tried speaking to Damyanti but was unable to take her out of the blow. She was deeply shocked and angry, angry with her own self, angry that she had allowed herself to live for many years in a world that was a figment of her wishful thinking. She had failed to read that the world that her grandfather so often spoke about, the Dacca and Bengal that he always assured her of, had died with him. She was angry at being naïve, of not having paid heed to the constant warning of Gautam, of not having read so many signals on so many occasions. She was angry at having trusted men who came with knives and axes behind her, many of whose brothers and uncles were given employment by her uncles and cousins. She was not able to bear the thought that a bunch of men, driven by greed, animosity, and hatred were deciding that she didn't have place in the land that she had always thought was hers. And for these reasons, she blamed herself for the death of Radha and other members of her family. She did not utter a single word for the next three days, hardly slept, and just sat in a corner of the crammed tent.

Then, on the fourth day, she walked up to Gautam and asked, 'Gautam, is your Bombay offer still open? Can we move there?'

'Daam, things may get normal. We will leave for Dacca after that.'

'I do not want to go to Dacca. I want to live outside Bengal. Please take me somewhere else. I will go mad if I go back. I cannot live in surroundings that will remind me of all that I have seen in the past one week. My head will burst thinking of what our sweet Radha went through, how *Kaku's* entire family was butchered, how the utterly religious *Chota Kaka* had to renounce his religion to embrace Islam, and how hundreds have become fatherless and widows.' She held Gautam's hand tightly and started sobbing. The sobs turned to wails, and she pleaded, 'Please take me away from all this.'

'But Daam, our house in Dacca...'

She interrupted him, 'No Gautam, please... please...'

Gautam hugged her tightly as he wiped her tears with one hand and caressed her head with the other. He wrote three letters from the camp that day.

The first one was to Arup's wife. He mentioned the riot and that they were safe. He briefly mentioned that he might have a job offer outside Dacca and would let her know soon. He requested her to take care of his sons till they were back.

He wrote a second letter to the administrator at Bhartiya Vidya Bhavan asking him if the position was still vacant.

And a third letter to his friend Bisesar Nath Singh. Bisesar and he were together in Presidency College. Although not a part of the same group, they were close friends and had remained in touch. Bisesar was a lecturer in the science department of Patna College. The department, established in 1927, was later converted to Patna Science College. Founded in 1863, Patna College, with a large teaching staff, was one of the oldest institutes in the sub-continent. He wrote about the riot. He also mentioned Damyanti's need to live outside Bengal.

He received a prompt reply from Bhartiya Vidya Bhavan expressing regret that the position had been filled.

In a few days, he received a letter from Indrani *boudi*, Arup's wife. The letter, incoherent, but full of emotion, seemed to be written in haste and with a lot of worry and fear. She promised to take care of the boys as her own children.

After a week, he received a letter from Bisesar. His family were landlords in Central Bihar, one with considerable influence. Saddened and pained to learn what his friend had gone through and that they might need to make a fresh beginning, he wrote, 'Gautam, I have a large house in Patna and a part of the house is unoccupied. Please take the next available train, come, and live with us. Please get the kids with you.' Towards the end, he mentioned, 'I have spoken to the Principal of Patna College, Gorakh Nath Singh. The college needs bright teachers. He seemed very interested in you. Damyanti *bhabhi* can teach at Prince of Wales Medical College in Patna. Singh Sir has promised to help. Gautam, I am sure things will be fine and Damyanti *bhabhi* may eventually want to go back to Dacca. But, should you all want to build things afresh, Patna is a good place. Both of you can work here.'

Gautam discussed the offer with Damyanti. They took

the train to Patna. Gautam got a job at Patna College, and with a little support from Gorakh Nath, Damyanti got a teaching assignment at the medical college. In a month, Gautam got his sons to Patna.

***

India became independent on August 15, 1947. It was not the India that Damyanti had dreamt of. The country was split into two; so was Bengal. The western part of Punjab, the region beyond that, and the eastern part of Bengal became a new country — Pakistan. Dacca was now part of Pakistan.

India was mutilated. Damyanti's Bengal cut into two pieces.

There were riots and bloodshed. People died in thousands and many were rendered homeless. Both Hindus and Muslims migrated from one side of the border to the other, robbed of home, wealth, and ties to their motherland. The Partition saw one of the largest mass migrations of mankind.

On August 15, at the stroke of the midnight hour, the nation was glued to radios and transistors to hear Pandit Nehru's speech. There was jubilation everywhere. India was becoming an independent nation after more than two centuries of British rule, and a democracy for the first time in her long history. But one lady chose to stay away, lying on her bed in Patna, her newfound home, eyes fixed on the ceiling, lost in thought, in mourning, struggling to forget the past — pleasant and unfortunate, and wanting to make an absolutely new start to life.

Damyanti was hurt. She felt dismembered just like her motherland. But she had to move on, for Gautam, her sons, and Arup's daughter. She was determined to build things afresh, work hard, and ensure that the past did not cast its shadow on the future of the children.

She wanted to forget Dacca. She was angry with its people and the city. She would obliterate every little memory associated with it.

PART II

O majhi tor naam jani naaa
Ami dak dimu kare...ami daak dimu kaare?
O majhi tor naam jani naaa...

O boatman I don't know your name
Whom would I call...Whom would I call?
O boatman I don't know your name...

Chapter 8

In the month of October, uncertain what the future would hold for them in Dacca, Indrani and her daughter joined Damyanti's family in Patna. With most of her family now away from Dacca, it had become difficult for Arup's widow to manage her daily life. In such trying times she could only depend on her sister-in-law Damyanti, and the latter was only too happy to welcome the family of the brother she had always loved dearly. Gautam rented a sufficiently spacious house in Kadamkuan, a well-regarded residential area, for the seven members.

Damyanti's sons Soumitro and Sumanta were admitted to St. Michael's High School. Established in 1858, it was one of the oldest and most-reputed missionary schools in eastern India. Sahana, Indrani's daughter, was admitted to Mount Carmel School, an equally reputed school.

Damyanti and Gautam did not take much time to adjust to Patna. The city and its people welcomed them with open arms. Gautam gained repute as a professor of economics and an expert on the subject. He was inducted into the advisory panel of the Bihar government to advise them on economic affairs. Damyanti was acknowledged as a bright professor of medicine and a very good physician. She practised at her home in the evenings and was popularly called *Daktar Didi*. She never accepted money from the poor, vehemently refusing any such offer. Initially, it was people from her neighbourhood — cooks, watchmen, servants, shop workers, etc. who visited her. As word spread around, their friends, families, and acquaintances all over Patna started visiting. The affection with which she treated each of her patients and the comfort that they had with her brought them to her clinic, and every time they came, they carried homemade sweets for her to compensate for the fee. Damyanti made it a point to always take the sweets or bowl of *kheer* and insisted that the entire family share it. She knew it came with heartfelt wishes and the most sincere blessings.

Damyanti and Gautam were invited to book launches, charity events, social causes, and discussions. They consciously kept away from political parties. The Communists felt that the couple belonged to their group, given their antecedents and social leanings. The Hindu Mahasabha believed they were an obvious party for the two after all that they had gone through in Noakhali. And the Congress, aware that many of Damyanti's family members were donors and strong party members in Calcutta, believed they were an obvious choice. While the couple politely refused invitations to join any political party, they participated in all social causes, irrespective of the party that organized it. They were loved and respected by one and all.

With time, people stopped discussing Dacca and East Bengal in Damyanti's presence. She showed complete detachment on the subject and place. She went to Calcutta to meet family members on all the important occasions, but avoided being there during *Durga Puja* and *Lakshmi Puja*. If there was ever an article on East Pakistan in the *Indian Nation*, an English daily, she never read beyond the headline.

Dacca — where she had always thought she belonged, the only place she had dreamt of living in, where she had built the home which probably still existed, where her sons were born, and where her dear sister and friend Samina lived — didn't seem to exist at all for her.

In her heart, however naively, she still believed that the majority of Muslims never wanted Hindus to leave East Bengal. She often wondered how a small group of people, strayed, selfish, and greedy, could impose their views on the majority. Why didn't the majority gather courage to voice their views? Why did they remain passive? After all, almost everyone had loved-ones on either side, and they knew that Partition would only lead to losses, financial and emotional. How could an English judge, who had no understanding of the sub-continent, a man who had never stayed in India, and did not understand the ties between people that existed across the Partition lines he drew, be given the task to divide a country? Didn't he realize that the simple line that he drew on the map went through the hearts of many, tearing and bleeding them?'

But these thoughts remained within her. People who knew her were convinced that she had left the past behind; and those who had not known her could never tell the agony that she went through. No one knew the anguish that went with her to bed most nights, how she was failing to erase Dacca from her memory.

For the most part, she kept herself busy with work and the three kids. She treated Sahana as her own daughter, one that she had always wanted. Eventually, in 1950, Gautam's mother passed away, never quite recovering from the trauma in Noakhali. At times, she would recede into the past with such fervour that she'd start calling for her daughter, Radha. She would often insist for water from the family well, and on such occasions, only Gautum could pacify her. He would fetch water from outside and tell his mother that it was from the well. He would sit at her feet and patiently talk to her. And the moment his mother regained her senses, she would cry loud, beating her chest. On such nights, Gautam would sleep beside his mother.

By 1958, the couple had constructed their own house in Kadamkuan, a few lanes away from the house of Jay Prakash Narayan. By this time, their eldest son Soumitro had moved to Oxford University on a scholarship. Education was given a lot importance in their house.

In the summer of 1958, he was home on a break from college.

'*Maa*, did you know someone named Samina in Dacca?' Damyanti was startled with Soumitro's question.

Not wanting to answer, but curious to know where he had heard about Samina, she acted as if she was trying to think hard before murmuring a quick yes.

'You never tell us about your life in Dacca. All we know is from our cousins.'

'There is hardly anything to tell. You know how boring your mother is. Also, I am getting old and my memory is fading,' Damyanti faked a laugh.

'On hearing your name, Razaq told me that his mother has a friend named Damyanti, who she never tires talking about. We were wondering if the two of you are friends.'

'Who is Razaq?'

'Oh! I forgot to tell you. He is studying history at Oxford and lives a few rooms away from mine. He is from Dacca. His mother's name is Samina and his father is a lieutenant colonel in the army. His uncle, Salim, is a prominent politician in Dacca. We get along really well.'

Upon hearing the names that she had tried to banish from her memory, Damyanti froze. Then nearly losing her balance to dizziness, she dragged herself to the edge of the bed and sat down.

'*Maa*, are you fine?' Soumitro rushed to her side.

'Yes, Soumi. Nothing much, low BP. I will cook fish for you today.' She was in haste to change the topic. She avoided discussing Razaq and his family with Soumitro for the remaining part of his stay. In a month, he went back to England, leaving behind an anxious mother.

He dropped a letter to his mother within a week of reaching England. After a few lines of initial greetings and informing her of his safe arrival, he wrote with palpable excitement, 'Razaq's mother was very happy to hear about you. His mother's friend also has two sons with the same names as us. He tells me that her tears refused to stop when he told her about us, and she has been telling everyone that she has at last found her friend. She requested for our Patna address and I have given it to him. *Maa*, you never told us that you had someone so dear in Dacca. In fact, I don't even remember you mentioning her at all...'

Damyanti got up from her chair, locked her room, and sat on the floor with the letter in her hand. Her head between her knees, tears flowing like River Padma.

As she had expected, in less than a month she received a letter through airmail. It was brief.

Dear Damyanti,

Our sons are close friends in Oxford. I learnt about you from my son.

I have been trying for many years to find a friend lost to unfortunate circumstances. Everything that he mentioned about you matches with her. I am sure the coincidence cannot be so high. But if you are not my Paki, I am sorry for the trouble.

Please do reply. I will be waiting anxiously to hear back from you.

Your Samina

Damyanti controlled her tears as she saw her patients outside. With moist eyes and hands that had grown numb, she struggled to fold the letter and keep it in her bag.

She had informed her relatives in Calcutta not to share her address with anyone from Dacca. The umbilical cord was cut, and in her mind any contact would only cause pain and agony. She had decided to stay away and did not reply to Samina's letter.

In two months, another letter arrived, not very different from the first one. But this time it came with a request for postal acknowledgement, and the compounder received it. He signed the acknowledgement slip, handed it over to the postman and placed the letter neatly on her table.

She read the letter, cried in the confines of her clinic, but did not reply.

A month after receiving the signed acknowledgement slip, Samina wrote her third letter; this time a long one. The letter read —

'My dearest Paki,

From the time you left Dacca, there has not been a day when I have not missed you. The time that we spent together and the dreams that we saw for our families have always been fresh in my mind. Paki, I am not as intelligent and emotionally strong as you, and could never overcome this sudden, unfortunate, and agonizing change that we had to face. There are nights when I cry without a moment of sleep.

Don't I know how you feel being uprooted from Dacca? May Allah's curse fall on all who were involved in the inhuman, deplorable, and disgusting acts at Noakhali. As Salim da says, the small minority of selfish and unintelligent people, easily swayed by rhetoric and false depictions have permanently damaged the beautiful social fabric that we always took pride in.

Paki, I was expecting a reply from you immediately on receipt of my letter. I have been waiting impatiently to hear from you. I wait for letters from Razaq hoping that he would write something about you. My son thinks that his mother has gone mad. I told Razaq to tell Soumitro about how I had wished that he was born a girl and how I had requested you that if a girl was born to you I would get her married to Bashir and take her as my daughter-in-law; Bashir, who was like a son to you, who loved being in your lap more than being in mine. How the two of us had wished that our families became one.'

Samina continued to write, pouring her pent up emotions on sheets of paper.

   '*...Life has been very difficult for us. We have become second-class citizens in our own country. We are under pressure to adopt Urdu as a language instead of Bengali. Paki, our rich Bengali literature may get replaced with Urdu; Bengali language may become alien to our future generations. At times, I feel it is better that you are away from all this. Paki...*'

Damyanti read and reread the last paragraph, unable to comprehend. She had kept herself away from discussions on East Bengal, now East Pakistan. She had seen clips in newspapers, but had never read beyond the headlines, assuming them to be nothing more than political stunts. The fact that it could impact her loved ones had always escaped her.

'Second class citizens! Urdu may replace Bengali, and gradually the language may die!' The words echoed in her mind. Troubled, she went to bed, but could not sleep. Gautam was away in Delhi with government officials. And so, restless, she got up from bed early in the morning and sat down to write a letter to Samina.

   '*...Samin, I am extremely sorry that I didn't reply earlier. For the last decade and more I have tried to remain away from anything even remotely connected to Dacca and East Bengal; not because of anger, but fear. Fear that the memories may drive me insane. I can only tell you that I have failed. There hasn't been a day when an incident has not reminded me of Dacca, opening a floodgate of memories* *and causing unimaginable pain…*

A young woman came to consult me this evening accompanied with her three-year-old daughter. Her daughter ran and started rolling on my front lawn, reminding me of how Salma as a child would refuse to lie on the cot, preferring to roll on the grass in my lawn, and how the two of us would have to plead her to get up with inducement of Payas or hot Nimki. And how the same Salma would take care of Soumitro and Sumanta as a young girl, how the two of us would chat with abandon that she would take care of the boys.'

She wrote about her family, detailing achievements of her sons and Sahana. She wanted to share all that had happened in the last twelve years and words flowed like water. She mentioned about the passing away of Gautam's mother, how she could never recover from the shock of Noakhali, or accept any other place as home.

'…I have not kept myself updated on the developments in East Bengal. Samin, I fail to understand how one can be treated as a second-class citizen in his own country. And I am shocked to hear that Urdu could replace Bengali. The thought of Bengali dying as a language in East Bengal pains me…' Damyanti continued.

The letter started a series of letters between the two friends. Every letter that Samina received brought her happiness and peace. But letters that Damyanti received only increased her anxiety and anger.

On her return from *Karim-Dinanath Bangla Sahitya Sammelan,* Samina found the letter neatly placed on Iqbal's table. The literary event started by Salim in memory of the two doyens of Dacca and as a celebration of the relationship between the two families was an effort to nurture talent in Bengali literature. It was also a tribute to Sujoy and Dinanath, but for whom their business would not have flourished. Salim and his family acknowledged that the foundation of their business, one of the largest industrial houses in Dacca, was actually laid by Sujoy Ranjan Ghosh.

She was overjoyed on receiving the letter, and sat down to reply the same night.

'...*Paki, we had been to* Karim-Dinanath Bangla Sahitya Sammelan *today. Salim* da *has been hosting this event annually for almost a decade. It nurtures talent in Bengali literature and is his tribute to the relationship that our families have had for generations. I have been attending this event since its inception. Every time Salim* da *sees me at the event, he reminds me of my disinterest in books and studies as a child, and how you would make me sit and patiently explain things. Paki, you were brilliant in studies, smart as a child; no wonder you studied to be a doctor. Do you remember how Bashir would run away to you when I tried teaching him, insisting that he would only learn from his* Masi.

Actually, dada *started this event after the row over the national language. Within months of independence, Urdu was ordained as the only official language. Even in Bengal people were forced to abandon Bengali for Urdu, media and schools were instructed to exclusively use Urdu. Bengali was removed from currency and stamps. The Pakistan Public Service Commission removed Bengali from the list of approved subjects, making it difficult for Bengali students to compete for government jobs. This when only three percent of people in Pakistan speak Urdu, whereas fifty-five percent speak Bengali.*

Though both the languages were eventually accepted as state languages after continuous protest for many years, Dada *still views the legislation with suspicion. He believes that the* Sahitya Sammelan *will not only keep interest in the language alive, but will also act as a pivot for protest in future…*

Paki, do you remember Farhan? I met him at the Sahitya Sammelan *today. Do you remember how you had shouted at him and argued fiercely during Tapan's younger brother's wedding? How you had chided him on his strong views in favour of a separate country for Muslims and how I had to drag you away fearing that you might slap him. I was tempted to ask him how he feels about that idea now. But he appeared so lost and troubled, a shadow of the young rebel that he was. He is working as a professor in Dacca University. He was remembering Gautam and you fondly.'*

Samina continued to write on the language crisis in the subsequent letters — how protests were brutally crushed and how insensitive people were towards the Bengali speaking population, a majority in Pakistan. She wrote about her fear of the planned and manipulated death of the language.

In a year, when Governor Abdul Monem Khan banned Rabindranath Tagore's songs on Radio Pakistan and announced that celebrating his birthday would be treated as an act of defiance, every sentence that Samina wrote weeped and every word that Damyanti read brought tears to her eyes.

'*Kobiguru's* songs banned in Bengal? His birthday treated as an act of defiance? How could such things happen in Dacca?' She stood in front of the window with the letter crumpled in her clenched fist and several questions plaguing her mind. 'Ma Durga, may these *outsiders* be cursed!'

Damyanti's attempt at forgetting Dacca had failed. The façade that she had built melted when she heard that the people who she loved were being persecuted and the culture that she took pride in was being targeted and systematically erased.

Samina's letters became a window to the world that Damyanti had left behind but continued to long for.

Damyanti's house in Dacca was occupied by a Muslim family from the United Provinces, and her father's house was occupied by a migrant family from Calcutta. The unauthorized occupation of the two houses disturbed Samina. On her insistence, Iqbal had gone to speak to the occupants. He argued that the families might return and the houses still belonged to Gautam and Arup. The occupants, aware of Arup's death and the tragedy that the family had faced at Noakhali, were sure that the families would not return and refused to vacate. Iqbal, a decorated military officer, then a major in the army, requested government officials for help and support. He argued on several occasions, but failed. Not one to give up easily, Samina tried to retain the house herself, hoping that the families might return some day. But, in a few months the occupants managed to obtain relevant legal papers to prove that they were the real owners of the two houses.

Iqbal and Samina had tried very hard, and so had some of their friends. They felt powerless in the new environment and believed that the system was more just when the English had governed Bengal.

A large number of Urdu speaking people from north India, *Mohajirs*, and affluent educated Muslims from West Bengal, who were not native Bengalis but had come along with the Mughal armies and settled there, migrated to East Pakistan. The power shifted to them. Even in East Pakistan, Urdu speaking people were preferred for government jobs. The native Bengalis had become powerless in their own land.

Samina wrote about her fight with the occupants and authorities, '...*Paki, power rests with people who have come from outside. We are considered lesser Muslims and told that we need to shed our 'Bengaliness'. The Bengali script is derived from Sanskrit, our culture is similar in some ways to our Hindu brothers and sisters, we do not follow the Islamic calendar and celebrate Poila Baishakh as New Year. As per the Government, they need to 'Islamise' us. They cannot understand our love and respect for our language and culture.*

Paki, who are they to question and judge if I am a complete Muslim? Don't they understand that religion is a matter of faith and not about the language one speaks or the way he lives? How can religion be biased to the language and medium that literature is expressed in?

With the letter in her hand, Damyanti cried with disgust, despair, and helplessness. She had kept herself away from any news about Dacca, still harboured hatred towards people who were responsible for her leaving Dacca, but her love for the place had remained intact. Dacca was beyond the bunch of vile men who were responsible for partition and bloodshed. It was the land nurtured by her great-grandfather and grandfather, the land that had given her so many pleasant memories, a place that was like a mother to her. And now, her mother's modesty was being outraged. The feeling of anger that she felt now was not very different from that she had felt in Noakhali.

By the end of 1965, Razaq and Soumitro had secured teaching assignments at Oxford and Cambridge University respectively. Razaq was married to an English girl. Soumitro was engaged to the daughter of a family friend, owners of a large publishing house in Patna. Damyanti's younger son, Sumanta, had completed his graduation from St. Stephen's College, Delhi, and had qualified for the Indian Administrative Service in his first attempt. He was posted as a Deputy Collector in Uttar Pradesh. His wife, Sarika, a batch mate in IAS, was posted in the adjoining district. Damyanti's niece, Sahana, had completed her MBBS and MD in Obstetrics and Gynaecology from

Darbhanga Medical College. She had applied to the Royal College of Physicians in London. Her husband, an officer in the Indian Foreign Service (IFS), was posted in the Indian embassy there.

Bashir, Samina's eldest son, had moved back to Dacca from his initial posting at Rawalpindi. The young captain was blessed with two sons, cynosure of their grandma's eyes. Samina's daughter, Salma, had completed medicine from Dacca Medical College and Hospital, established in 1946. She was practising medicine in the same clinic in which Damyanti had practised many years back. Engulfed with emotion that she could not get the illegal occupants to vacate Damyanti's house, Samina had bought the clinic from the original owners.

Any other time, such accomplishments would have been a matter of great celebration for both families.

Around this time, Iqbal, in line to be a colonel, was superseded for promotion and asked to report to a Punjabi officer, a few years junior to him. The army was completely dominated by officers from Punjab. In fact, only three percent of them were from East Pakistan. Iqbal felt that the national government and the army did not trust officers from East Pakistan. He had been very upset.

Disturbed at the humiliation meted to Iqbal, Samina poured her heart to her friend. But she ended the letter with optimism.

'...*Paki, amidst gloom and despair, I see some hope. Iqbal and I accompanied* Dada *to meet Mujib, leader of the Awami League. He has just been released from prison by the government. He demonstrates strong determination to restore the Bengali pride and plans to fight for autonomy of East Bengal.* Dada *had gone to receive him when he was released. He was telling me that if the number of people that had assembled to see him is any measure of the support and enthusiasm that each of them exhibit, the Government of Pakistan will be forced to listen to us. I pray to Allah that he gives Sheikh Mujib the strength that he may need.'*

The Awami League had emerged as the largest party in East Pakistan, a representative voice of all Bengalis.

Iqbal's visit to Sheikh Mujib's house had not gone unnoticed by the army. That he had accompanied only to give company to his brother-in-law was never understood. No one bothered to ask him about the purpose of his visit. It was assumed that Lieutenant Colonel Iqbal, a man of unimpeachable integrity, was working against the government. It was also presumed that Bashir's movement to Dacca was as a part of a larger plan. The two were put under constant vigil after that day.

Meanwhile, India too was undergoing changes. Indira Gandhi, the only daughter of Pandit Nehru, was elected as Prime Minister of India in 1966. Damyanti, who had lost interest in politics, now suddenly read the news with a lot of curiosity. A woman as Prime Minister! Initially dubbed as a *'Gungi Gudiya'* ('Dumb Doll'), Indira Gandhi began asserting herself in matters of party and policies.

The country needed capital for industry and infrastructure, and multi-fold increase in branches of banks in rural areas. In order to enable this, the government needed a large say in the movement of funds and operations, which was not possible with banks in private hands. In July 1969, in spite of opposition from several sections, Indira Gandhi took the bold step of nationalizing fourteen commercial banks.

She was planning to nationalise coal mines and abolish Privy Purse accorded to the royal families. The power and steel plants needed more coal and infusion of capital was required to increase output. The owners were reluctant to put in additional capital. Also, the number of labourers employed in coal mines was very high, and at several places the employment conditions were poor and favourable to the owners.

Damyanti had begun admiring Indira Gandhi for her courage and determination. She would keenly observe her actions and statements, and respected her political acumen. Indira's actions appealed to her socialist sensibilities. She read every article written about her with interest and affection.

The situation in Dacca was rapidly deteriorating. Several members of the Awami League and Left parties mooted the idea of separation from Pakistan into a different country. In no time, the thought permeated to general mass. People knew that independence could not be achieved without external help, and who better than India to seek help from.

East Pakistan was simmering with anger and discontent. The oppressive method of the government managed to curb agitation but left permanent scars on Bengalis.

Completely glued onto the happenings in Dacca and East Pakistan, Damyanti was living a life of fluctuating emotions, sometimes of hope, but mostly of despair. Every piece of news that reached her through Samina's letter, radio, and newspaper left her anxious. She would wait for the newspaper hawker and rush to check the headlines the moment it was delivered. Absence of any news would leave her restless.

When the new Army Chief, General Yahya Khan, announced that elections for the Pakistan National Assembly would be held by the end of 1970, she was filled with hope. She was aware that the Pakistan National Assembly had 300 seats, out of which 162 seats were in East Pakistan. The Awami League needed to win 151 seats out of those 162 to form government, a difficult but not impossible task. She knew that such a win would mean that the Prime Minister and cabinet ministers of Pakistan would be Bengalis, and it could end the tyranny on her people. She began praying for an absolute majority for the Awami League in the elections.

The letters between Damyanti and Samina in those

months were full of happiness and optimism in anticipation of a win. Her hope was further strengthened with the news that the Awami League won 160 seats, a clear majority in the National Assembly.

Damyanti was waiting for Samina's letter after the win in election. And as expected, every word of the letter echoed her excitement.

'...Paki, did we ever imagine that we would have our own government in Pakistan? A government completely of Bengalis? Dada says that once the Awami League forms government the party would amend the Constitution to make it more equitable. Sheikh Mujib will be our new Prime Minister and everyone says that Dada may be minster in charge of education. Paki, my sister, our difficult days may be over...'

Salim, a minister! How proud she felt. Had she ever imagined that the young boy who would often pamper her, ensure that all her demands were met, would one day be a minister of his country. She had always believed that he would achieve great heights, he stood out from the rest, but becoming a minister was dreamlike. How she wished she were in Dacca to see him in all his glory. 'He had dedicated his life to struggle for his people, and Bengal would be lucky to have a man as fair and capable as him for a Minister', she thought. She walked across to the portrait of Ma Durga, thanked her, and prayed for Salim and her brothers and sisters in Bengal.

But Damyanti's hope quickly turned to despair when

the Awami League was not allowed to form government. The military and bureaucracy, dominated by people and politicians from West Pakistan, rejected the idea of a government run only by the Awami League. Bhutto wanted a joint government and a share in power, but Mujib rejected that. He proclaimed that he and his party would boycott the assembly session.

In this environment of gloom, despair, and anger, Damyanti encountered a reason to cheer. Every year on Guru Nanak Jayanti and Guru Gobind Singh Jayanti, Damyanti and Gautam visited the Patna Saheb Gurudwara for *paath* and *langar*. On one such visit, Damyanti met a person named Paramjit Dussanj. The Dussanj family owned a mid-sized hotel called Sagar Hotel, a restaurant, a large grocery shop on Boring Road, and a car garage in Patna.

On their return from the *gurudwara,* they stopped at Paramjit's house for a cup of tea. As she sat on the sofa, Damyanti's eyes fell on a photograph on the opposite wall. The photograph, in a beautiful wooden frame, had turned yellow with age and was a little crumpled. Out of curiosity, she walked to the photograph. The photograph had three men standing, their names — Davinder Dussanj, Sujoy Ranjan Ghosh, and Abhishek Talukdar; the name of the studio, 'Bourne & Shepherd, Calcutta'; and the year 1863 all written below. She looked at the man standing in the middle, tall and straight, and then looked at the name,

'Sujoy Ranjan Ghosh.' Unmistakably, this was her great-grandfather. While she did not have a photograph of her great-grandfather, she did have an old portrait. The resemblance was uncanny. During the discussion, she learnt that Paramjit's grandfather had migrated to Patna from Dacca. Overwhelmed with emotion that the two families had come close after a couple of generations, she started crying.

From that day, Damyanti often went to Paramjit's house in the evenings. In him, she found her connection to Dacca, a connection that, though not remotely close to the one with Samina, was at least not so distant.

Chapter 9

As the deadlock increased in Dacca, Damyanti's anxiety grew. Once again, the Leftists started demanding a separate nation. In anticipation of a worse situation, the military increased its vigilance on people they had earmarked, and that included Lt. Col. Iqbal and his son, Captain Bashir.

In order to negotiate a settlement, Gen. Yahya and Bhutto flew to Dacca in the middle of March. While Yahya was willing to sign the declaration for autonomy of East Pakistan, Bhutto and several others were opposed to it. On Mach 23, the Awami League presented a draft for declaration of autonomy to Gen. Yahya with a demand that it should be issued within forty-eight hours. Before the expiry of the deadline, Gen. Yahya flew back to West Pakistan without informing the leaders of the Awami League. And before he left, he issued an order for movement of more troops to East Pakistan and attack the people involved in the agitation.

That same evening, people took out a march in Dacca with the flag of *Bangladesh*.

The next day, officers and leaders suspected of working against the government were arrested. Captain Bashir was picked from duty and taken into custody. He was charged with treason and put in an isolation ward within the cantonment. Major Durrani and Major Niyazi were given the task to interrogate him to find out details about the plans of the Awami League and the kind of weapons the protestors had piled. Major Niyazi, who Bashir had saved risking his own life in the 1965 war, had been telling his superiors that he suspected Bashir of training the rebels. In these times of deep hatred, kindness of any kind was long forgotten.

Lt. Col. Iqbal went from one officer and bureaucrat to another to find the whereabouts of his missing son. No one seemed to have any information of the missing captain. He pleaded with his officers; almost sure that Bashir might have been put in custody. He professed the innocence of his son, but did not receive any help.

It had been four days with no news of Bashir when one afternoon his body was found beside a railway track in a secluded area. The body had several cuts. Three fingers were cut off, and out of the seven remaining, four did not have nails on it. There was a gunshot right in the middle of the forehead.

Bashir's body, wrapped in a black cloth, was placed on

the floor of the living room. His wife, not having recovered from the shock of her husband's sudden and brutal death, was lying unconscious in the adjacent room. Samina, sitting near the feet of her son's dead body, was inconsolable. Bashir's elder son was howling. The younger son was standing next to his grandfather, holding his finger, not able to comprehend the enormity of the tragedy. Salim, along with Salma's husband were busy making arrangements to carry the body for burial. An effort was made to convey the sad news to Razaq, but with clear instructions that he should stay in England and not leave for Dacca.

Around five hundred people — family members, neighbours, friends, colleagues from army, and students from Dacca University — had gathered outside Iqbal's house. There was gloom and anger all around. Bashir's body was lifted and placed in a small truck to be taken for burial. The men present walked along the truck. As the truck moved out of the neighbourhood to the main road, news started spreading that Lt. Col. Iqbal's son, a brave and loyal soldier, nephew of the loved and respected leader Salim, was brutally tortured and killed. Though there had been a huge crackdown on civilians and army men, people came out in large numbers to share grief and joined the group to go to the graveyard. In no time, the small group became a large procession. People were shouting slogans for the young soldier and for avenging his death. The many students in the procession insisted that the body be taken via Dacca University. Fearing that the army may crackdown on the procession, Salma's husband was not in favour of taking a detour, but had to yield to the students. As the procession reached the university building amidst high sloganeering, the resident students came out of the hostels. The news spread fast about the brutal torture and death of Salim's nephew, and on seeing Salim, the students requested him to speak a few words and address the gathering. The procession halted at the main gate of Dacca University.

The students lifted Salim on to the boundary wall. The slogans stopped and there was complete silence.

'Today, *Bangladesh* has lost a brave and young son to the atrocities of the Pakistan Army,' Salim's deep voice could be heard by all.

Hearing Salim mention *Bangladesh*, and not Pakistan or East Pakistan, or for that matter Bengal, the crowd went into frenzy. The word *Bangladesh* had an almost euphoric influence on everyone present. Salim was barely heard after that through undying applause and slogans.

On his return home, Iqbal called Samina and his daughter-in-law into a room. Salim was also present. The four of them had an intense discussion. After the discussion, he called for his grandsons. He took them on his lap, stroked their head with love, and spoke to them. 'My brave darlings, we have anxious times ahead with enemy all around us. Your *Dadu* needs to go to fight them, and so your *Dadima* will take you to a safer place for a few months. I promise you that you will return to a truly independent Bangladesh, a nation that will be yours, where you will live with respect and without fear, and where our Bengali literature and culture will not only be protected but also flourish.' Not able to completely comprehend what their grandfather was saying, the kids just hugged him.

The next day, Samina went to a few neighbours and informed them that the family would leave for Chittagong to visit a cousin who had not been keeping well. But, along with her daughter-in-law and grandsons, she took the train to Sylhet and not Chittagong. The family planned to stay with Parineeta till things became fine. Parineeta was surprised and overjoyed to see her friend at her doorstep. The two friends hugged and wept as they exchanged news about their families.

The next day, Salim and Iqbal went to the market, and from there left in disguise to their respective destinations. Salim sneaked out of the country and went to Calcutta to his colleagues. Together, they formed the provisional government of Bangladesh based out of Calcutta.

In addition to the official Bangladesh Forces, *Mukti Bahini* was set up with guerrilla forces. Lt. Col. Iqbal took the responsibility of commanding one such *Bahini* comprising mostly of retired soldiers and some civilians with an objective of destroying Pakistani establishments through guerrilla warfare.

In a few weeks, Damyanti received a letter from Soumitro. He had written to convey the tragic death of Bashir. He had also mentioned the condition in which the body was found. She read the letter many times, not wanting to believe what was written.

She slumped on the ground, trembling with pain and fear as several images of Bashir from his childhood flashed in her mind. Bashir was the first born among all the children of Samina and Damyanti, and hence an object of extreme anxiety and a recipient of immense love from the two. Damyanti was in medical college when he was born. She had rushed to Dacca the day she had received Samina's letter informing her of his birth. She wanted to see him, hold him close. He was named Bashir, 'one who brings good news', on her suggestion. He took his first step in front of her eyes. Whenever she was in Dacca, he would be with her. When Samina was pregnant with Salma, he lived with her in her house. She was an aunt, mother, and later a teacher to him. And for her, he was the elder brother to her two sons.

With tears and rage in her eyes, and the letter torn into pieces but still in her clenched fist, she was standing in her living room in front of the large portrait of Ma Durga. Her sister had lost her son in the most inhuman way. How she wished she was there, consoling and comforting her sister, like she had when Iqbal was missing during the war. Decades ago, a bunch of ugly men had taken away her right to live in eastern Bengal, and now, another bunch of equally ugly men had taken away the life of her young Bashir. She wanted punishment for these men, harsh and brutal. She wanted them humiliated, begging for mercy. These men were no different from the men thirsting for blood in Noakhali. She wanted to see them grovel, inflicted with deep wounds.

'Ma, please come down. Save my Bengal. Chase away these *outsiders*. Ma, avenge this injustice for me. Punish those who have murdered my young son,' her wail could be heard by the people outside.

Damyanti was not aware that her sister had to leave Dacca under almost similar circumstances as she had twenty years ago. Then, some people had decided that as a Hindu she didn't belong in eastern Bengal. Now, some men were deciding that her sister was not Muslim enough to stay. And Ma Durga knew, she often said, that her sister and she belonged to the city many times more than those who wielded power now and weapons then.

Damyanti wrote two letters to Samina after she learnt of Bashir's death, but did not receive any reply. Every day newspapers were flooded with news of atrocities by the Pakistan Army. She had started dreading headlines that spoke of mass killings, rape, or people fleeing in thousands to India. The border between India and East Pakistan had become very porous and many areas in Assam and Tripura were full of people who had taken shelter.

The movement of people did not seem to stop, causing a lot of strain on the local Indian governments. Every time she read news detailing such atrocities, she prayed to Ma Durga for her intervention, for punishment of the guilty, for correction of a colossal wrong.

The Pakistan Army launched Operation Searchlight immediately after Gen. Yahya Khan left for West Pakistan. Gen. Tikka Khan, the Martial Law Administrator of East Pakistan, issued instructions for indiscriminate killing of the rebels and destruction of all establishments sympathetic to the cause of Bengal. Two hundred thousand people were targeted and specific instructions were issued against Hindu rebels.

In the third week of June, Lt. Col. Iqbal and his troop attacked a Pakistani Army camp, the first of many to follow. One of the members of the troop was Farhan, a childhood friend of Tapan's brother and known to Damyanti during her college days. He had been a strong advocate of Partition along religious lines. After independence, he started working in Dacca with the planning department of Pakistan. Salman, whose protégé he had been, had moved into politics and business. Salman, a contemporary of Damyanti and Gautam in Calcutta University, had been an ardent advocate of division of India on religious lines and a rallying force for many Muslim students in the university. The couple, along with Tapan, had often been in bitter arguments with Salman on the need for one Bengal and one India.

Salman had built very good contacts with officers in the Pakistan Army. He began as a small civil contractor for the army, and quickly expanded his business to include supply of spares, repair of equipment, and construction of roads and bridges. He made a fortune for himself and later moved to Rawalpindi.

Farhan's job in the Planning Department exposed him to the unfair treatment meted to East Pakistan for budget and resource allocation. He often raised this with his superiors, but it fell on deaf ears. When he persisted with his demand, he was threatened with a transfer to an insignificant department. Aware of Salman's influence with army officers, he approached him many times for help. Salman would always hear him patiently and promise to speak to the authorities, but nothing happened. With time, Farhan realised that Salman never made any attempt to speak to anyone and had never intended to extend help to his motherland. In such situations, he would remember his discussions with Tapan *da* and Damyanti *di* during his college days; how he would strongly present his case for a separate country for Muslims and how Damyanti *di* would patiently try explain to him the futility of the idea; how passionately, with deep conviction, she advocated the idea of one Bengal and the Bengali identity.

Disillusioned, he resigned from Planning Department and started teaching in Dacca University. He was in Jagannath Hall, a dormitory for Hindu students, when the army entered Dacca University during Operation Searchlight.

Hindu students and professors were killed indiscriminately. Farhan was in a room with Bipin Pal, a Hindu student, one of his favourites. And before they could realise that they had been attacked, a gun wielding army man entered. Bipin could have jumped out of the window, but pushed Farhan to jump. And as Farhan landed on the ground, he heard the sound of a gunshot, the bullet that killed Bipin.

Devastated, angry, and wanting to avenge, Farhan joined *Mukti Bahini* in the next few weeks. He was a part of Lt. Col. Iqbal's troop and one of his most hardworking trainees.

***

Samina stopped writing to Damyanti, scared that her letters might get opened and read by Pakistani authorities. Damyanti's worry was increasing by the day; on one hand was the absence of communication from Samina and on the other were newspaper headlines screaming about death, rape, and destruction in East Pakistan.

'Gautam, Samina has always replied to my letters. It has been five months since I received her last letter, and more than two months since the last one I mailed. I am very worried about her.'

Gautam replied with his usual composure. 'Daam, I'm sure the family is fine, otherwise you would have heard something from Soumitro.'

'East Bengal is burning. Every day I read about mass killing, rapes, and people fleeing their homes. Sheikh Mujib has proclaimed independence, but in reality it continues to be a part of Pakistan. Gautam, when and how will these atrocities end?'

'Only with the intervention of a superpower.'

'You mean Maa Durga?' Damyanti asked looking at the large portrait of the Goddess on the wall.

Gautam started laughing. 'No, Daam. I mean we need a superpower like the USA to intervene and ask Pakistan to stop this genocide.'

'And, will the USA intervene?'

'I'm not sure, Daam. Nixon believes what Yahya tells him and needs him as a mediator to build his relationship with the Chinese.'

'What about the United Nations? Don't they see that thousands have been raped and killed and millions have fled their homes to India? Can the UN not recognize Bangladesh as an independent country?'

'The Chinese will veto any such initiative.'

'Yes, I know. I was speaking to Sahana's husband. Indira Gandhi has been lobbying with several countries to recognize Bangladesh as an independent nation. She has reached out to many to highlight the ugly human rights situation. Gautam, will India be able to help?'

'Maybe if the Indian army openly sides with Bangladesh and gets into a war with Pakistan.'

'It needs a lot of courage,' Damyanti spoke softly. 'Will any Indian leader have the strength to take such a bold step?'

'Yes, it needs a lot of courage. The cost that India is incurring towards millions of refugees may be higher than a war. But a war...' Gautam was lost in thoughts.

Damyanti looked at the portrait of Maa Durga, closed her eyes, and prayed.

After a few days, in the month of July, Henry Kissinger, Secretary of State of Nixon's government met Indira Gandhi at her residence. Indira Gandhi was determined to once again raise the issue of human rights violation in East Pakistan and the millions of refugees that had taken shelter in India. The next day, Damyanti read in the newspaper that General Maneckshaw had also attended breakfast in his army uniform. She understood that the presence of the general in uniform for a breakfast meeting was a subtle message from Mrs Gandhi to Kissinger of her intent to go to war if things were not brought under control.

'Brave and cunning,' she thought. She walked to the portrait of Maa Durga, folded her hands, and thanked her.

The situation continued to deteriorate, and along with that increased Damyanti's anxiety. In September, Damyanti received a letter from Biswanath requesting her to join

them in Calcutta for *Durga Puja*. It was also the twentieth death anniversary of his father, Mukul. She had consciously stayed away from *Puja* celebrations in Calcutta,
fearing old memories, but could not refuse an invitation
to attend the death anniversary of her uncle. She had very
fond memories of Mukul, who much like her grandfather,
Dinanath, had been a symbol of strength and power.

But there was also another reason why Biswanath was
insisting that she visit them but couldn't mention in the
letter.

She had her own reason for going to Calcutta. The
Ghosh family business had grown multi-fold and they
were one of the most prominent business families in Calcutta. Prasun, Biswanath's elder brother, had very good
relations with officials in the Indian government. And
Manas, son of Dinanath's third son, was close to several
businessmen in East Bengal. She had learnt from family
members that the two were the initial connect between
the Indian government and leaders of East Pakistan. The
government still relied on them and valued their inputs.
They were large donors to the cause, and a conduit to pass
funds to the Awami League and Mukti Bahini. She knew
that only her cousins could satisfy her curiosity, they would
have answers to many questions that kept troubling her.

Damyanti and Gautam reached Calcutta in the middle
of September and were welcomed with the usual warmth
and affection.

Aware that Manas had been actively engaged with the East Bengal rebels in Calcutta, she asked him when he was alone, 'Have you been to refugee camps? Manas, is the situation really bad? Or is it exaggerated by journalists?'

'It is very bad, Paki. I have been to Tripura, Assam, and northern Bengal. The state of refugees will make you cry. The help is completely inadequate.'

'When do you think they will be able to go back?'

'Some, never.'

'Never?' Damyanti exclaimed. 'Do you mean they will be refused entry? Or are you saying the situation will never become normal?'

'Most of the refugees, more than 80 per cent, are Hindus. Out of approximately 10 million refugees, only two million may be Muslims. Pakistan claims that the total refugee count is not more than two million and may refuse to take back the Hindu refugees.'

'Are you saying that people may not be able to return to their own country, the land of their ancestors?' Damyanti's pain was visible as she spoke.

'No one knows, Paki. And if this regime continues, they may not let them return.'

'Won't our brave Bengali rebels chase the Pakistanis out?'

'No, Paki. Neither are they equipped with enough

arms, nor do they have the numerical strength. While the Bengali rebels have been brave, they have only been successful in paralysing administration by damaging assets like electrical power stations, bridges, etc. Not only will it not help them achieve independence, but also the investment required to rebuild things may be very large.'

'So, Manas, is there no way to gain independence? Will this continue like this forever?'

Manas and his businessmen friends from East Bengal had been discreetly lobbying in the USA. The international media had increased its coverage on the genocide in East Pakistan and the growing number of refugees in India. Indira Gandhi had been touring several countries to convey to leaders the extent of refugee crisis. And, on her request, Jay Prakash Narayan was touring European countries to establish the cause of India and East Bengal. Nixon's administration was under pressure from internal and international forces.

'So, Manas, is there no way to gain independence? Will it continue like this forever?' Damyanti repeated her question.

'Maybe an India-Pakistan war.'

'And will India attack Pakistan for East Bengal? Won't China attack India if such a war breaks?'

'If the war happens in November or December, snow-capped mountains may prevent China from getting into the war. Paki, India may not attack Pakistan first, but if she escalates the situation in East Pakistan, the Pakistan army may end up making the mistake of the first strike. It will require a lot of courage for India to get into a full scale war.' And then he spoke softly, lest anyone else heard, 'Paki, Mrs Gandhi is our only hope. She is cunning and brave. I think she has a plan in her mind. I pray that Maa Durga gives her strength.'

On September 28, the *Mahastami* day, after completing *Pushpanjali,* the two cousins sat down with folded hands in front of the idol of Ma Durga. Damyanti prayed to the goddess for the safe return of all refugees, Hindus and Muslims, and the safety and happiness of all her Bengali brothers and sisters in East Bengal. She also prayed to the goddess that the army men responsible for the genocide be punished and justice be done. And above all, she prayed for happiness of her friend Samina and her family, who she had not heard from for a long time.

Manas prayed for independence of East Bengal, and only that.

After four days, on Saturday, October 2, Manas walked into Damyanti's room in the morning and spoke to her softly.

'Paki, let us have lunch at Blue Fox Restaurant on Park Street today.'

'No, Manas. I want to stay at home. I am feeling tired with so much *pandal* hopping in the last few days.'

'I have a surprise for you, Paki. You will thank me for it.'

'Manas, there is nothing on the menu in Blue Fox that I have not tasted. There is nothing there that can surprise me.'

'I have invited a guest and would like you to meet the person. But, you should act normal and not show any surprise or emotion.'

'Who is this person, Manas?'

'That's the surprise, Paki. And I'm not letting the name out.'

Damyanti smiled and agreed to the lunch. In her mind, she knew that this was possibly just one of Manas' hypes and hence was not expecting much.

The two cousins were seated in the corner table that was reserved for them. Damyanti was facing the main door and Manas was sitting opposite her.

Damyanti saw a tall man with thick grey hair, firm in posture, dressed in white *kurta* pyjama, a black Nehru jacket completely buttoned, walk inside. She rubbed her eyes, not able to believe what she was seeing. She could immediately recognise the person walking in. And seeing the change on her face, Manas looked back.

'Paki, be careful not to show any surprise or emotion.'

Salim, who was a part of the provisional government

of Bangladesh in Calcutta, walked in and sat next to Manas. Damyanti folded her hands in greetings, excused herself, and walked to the restroom. Locked there, she cried for fifteen minutes as old memories flashed in her mind. She wanted to rush back to the table and talk to him, yet found herself unable to take a few steps. She wiped her tears, composed her face, gathered strength, and walked back.

The three were in the restaurant for more than two hours. Damyanti was relieved to hear that Samina was safe. Salim told her about Bashir's torture and the extent of cruelty on Bengalis. Damyanti had scores of questions and Salim answered each one patiently, just like old times. He has not changed a bit, she thought. He was the same towards her, still willing to indulge her. She wanted to know about her house, the one that she had built with so much of love. She wanted every bit of detail possible about friends, patients, acquaintances, and places that she used to frequent. She had many questions on the war of independence. She asked each of these to gauge if the Bengali army would be able to win freedom. He answered each question, even those he would normally avoid answering.

But what she actually wanted to know was why he had remained a bachelor, why hadn't he settled down with a family, but she couldn't gather the courage. Would he have told her the truth? And what if the truth was what she suspected it to be, that Salim has taken her remark about getting married seriously and felt more for her than he showed, would she have been able to bear the burden of that truth?

The friends parted with a promise to meet again. In those two and a half hours, she had relived a large part of her life.

On reaching home, Damyanti hugged Manas and wept. Tears rolled down for old memories, the devastation in East Bengal, and the gratitude that she felt for her cousin.

By November, Indira Gandhi received mixed responses from the countries that she had visited. Everyone sympathised with the cause and the refugee crisis but refused to take a stand against Pakistan. Even the Soviets, an ally of India, did not want the issue of East Pakistan and the refugee crisis to be linked. She met Nixon too, but did not receive any assurance. In her subsequent meeting, she cold-shouldered him, thereby conveying a clear message. Strategically, she just discussed global foreign policy of the US and did not even bother to bring up the topic of East Pakistan.

Having understood that she might not get help from other nations, on her return, she gave instructions for escalation of armed support to the Bengali rebels. The Mukti Bahini now had army men from the Indian army disguised as Bengali soldiers fighting along with them. The strength of Iqbal's group doubled with men from the Indian Army.

His group had become adept at guerrilla warfare, responsible for destruction of Pakistani establishments.

The activities in various cantonments and temporary army camps increased from the second week of November. It was rumoured that these establishments were being stocked with new supplies of arms and armaments. The increased activity, constant training, and parades looked ominous. Groups like that of Iqbal's were tasked to attack such camps and destroy the pile of arms.

One such camp was headed by Major Niyazi, the officer suspected of killing Bashir. A plan was hatched to attack that camp. Iqbal had clearly instructed his team to only focus on destroying the arms and not engage in exchange of fire with army men who did not come in their way. The guerrilla attack was to be carried while the army men were on parade.

With the Indian army men joining Mukti Bahini, the Bangladesh Forces started attacking with renewed vigour, causing loss of lives and property. As the situation got worse, Yahya Khan declared emergency in Pakistan on 23rd November, and asked Pakistanis to prepare for war.

Two days later, at 11 am, while the army men were on parade, Iqbal's men stealthily moved to the area where the arms were kept. In the next ten minutes, they killed the guards and bombed the store. And before the men on parade could react, they were on their way back. While they were trying to escape, Farhan saw Major Niyazi standing in front of the troop. Emboldened by the presence of men from the Indian army in the group and engulfed by emotions of vengeance, he turned to fire at Major Niyazi. The first bullet missed the target, and he ran towards him to shoot from a closer range. The next two bullets from Farhan's guns went straight into the skull of Major Niyazi, and the latter fell on the ground dead. The bullets fired from the other side hit Farhan in his arms and legs. He fell on the ground, bruised and wounded. The men from Pakistan army were in a daze with the bombing of the storehouse and the death of their commander. A group of soldiers surged towards Farhan. Seeing them move towards Farhan, Sarat and Majid moved like lightning, risking their lives, picked him up, and ran towards the vehicle that was waiting. Sarat and Majid were shot too, but managed to escape.

Majid, a Muslim, was a soldier with the Indian army, and Sarat, a Bengali Hindu, was from Dacca. Struggling to remain conscious, but aware that the two had risked their own lives to save his, Farhan muttered softly, 'How I wish we had remained one! Partition was a big mistake, and I…' The words were drowned in the sound of bullets and explosion.

Farhan, a strong advocate of two nations on the basis of religion, was saved by two people — ironically, a Hindu from the land that he had wanted for Muslims, and a Muslim from the land that he had left for Hindus. And he, who had argued bitterly with Damyanti for a separate country for Muslims, killed an army officer of that very country, risking his life, to avenge the death of her adoptive son, Bashir.

While the attacks on Pakistani establishments had increased, it was only causing destruction of assets belonging to Bengal. Manas and his friends in the provisional government were growing impatient. They were worried that at this rate the state would be left with little resource and the investment required to rebuild the nation would be very high. Also, there was fear that worn out by continuous guerrilla warfare, with no concrete result coming out, the leaders might sign a compromised agreement for autonomy. And they knew that such an agreement would be temporary, an eyewash.

'A war between India and Pakistan may be the only way independence can be achieved,' Manas thought. He was aware that India would never attack Pakistan first, and if the war did not start in the next few weeks, it might not happen. And if the war didn't start, the destruction would continue indefinitely. He had learnt from various sources that India was completely prepared for war and the escalation in involvement in the east was bait for Pakistan. Manas was praying for Pakistan to make the mistake of attacking India.

On December 3, 1971, Mrs Gandhi was on her way back to Delhi from Calcutta. Still in air, she received a message through the pilot that the Pakistani air force had attacked northern India. She just smiled. She drove straight to the Army Headquarters from the airport. Gen. Maneckshaw briefed her on retaliatory actions and sought her permission to attack on the eastern front. Subsequent to her meeting, she met the entire cabinet.

Next day, India officially recognized Bangladesh as an independent country and the war with Pakistan was on. The Indian army fought the war with clinical precision. They captured the two major ports of Chittagong and Khulna and important river crossings and airfields, crippling the movement of Pakistani troops and cutting off any kind of reinforcements. The Pakistani army was isolated into small units, and with the help of local Bengali informers, these units were rapidly destroyed. The US government wanted China to threaten India with movement of their troops, but they refrained from doing so. When the Pakistani defeat looked imminent, the US army sent its aircraft carrier USS Enterprise to the Bay of Bengal to help them. In order to neutralise this, the Soviet Navy dispatched two groups of ships armed with nuclear missiles. They continued to trail the US ship in the Indian Ocean even after the war ended.

In thirteen days, on the 16th of December, Lt. Gen. A.A.K. Niazi, Commanding Officer of the Pakistan Army, signed the Instrument of Surrender, and more than 93,000 Pakistani soldiers were taken in as prisoners of war.

No one was happier than Damyanti that day. The defeat of Pakistan was the punishment that she had been praying for for the brutal massacre of her Bengali brothers and sisters, the insult that was inflicted on them for years, the murder of her Bashir. In her eyes, it was also a defeat of divisive forces, forces that had partitioned her Bengal and her country, men who had denied her the right to live peacefully in her Dacca. And, it was balm on her wounds of Noakhali, a wound that she knew would never completely heal.

The next day, newspapers carried a large photograph of Lt. Gen. Niazi signing the Instrument of Surrender. Damyanti cut that photograph neatly, got it framed in a beautiful wooden frame, and hung it on the wall next to the portrait of Maa Durga. And when the popular Jan Sangh leader, Atal Behari Vajpayee, called Indira Gandhi as an incarnation of Goddess Durga on the floor of the Parliament, no one could have agreed more.

That day, standing in front of the portrait of Maa Durga and the photograph of surrender beside it, Damyanti could only see good days ahead. Her country had a strong leader, popular amongst masses, and firm in her decisions. Her country of birth and a land that she loved and always would was free from the oppressive clutches of the *outsiders*. Not only was Bangladesh an independent country, but also had an extremely popular leader in Sheikh Mujibur Rehman as the head of state.

'Nothing can go wrong from here,' she thought. 'In

both countries people will live in harmony. My grandson Soumen and his friends and Samina's grandchildren will only see prosperity, peace, and freedom.'

She thanked Ma Durga and Mrs Gandhi, repeatedly, tears of gratitude in her eyes.

After many years, she slept well that night, deep and sound, with a sense of relief.

Damyanti's hope that nothing could go wrong quickly turned to gloom. The years ahead were again filled with pain. She would find herself in the same situations of helplessness and misery that she had experienced in the last few decades.

She would soon realise that it is not always borders that defined *outsiders*.

Chapter 10

If Damyanti had ever felt as thankful to anyone as she did to Ma Durga and Ma Kali, it was to the Indian army. She wanted to thank every soldier who had fought the Pakistan army, who had braved bullets from the enemy, had risked his life for her brothers and sisters or died fighting. In her mind, Lieutenant Prayag, who was returning to his sister's house in Patna after the war, represented the vast Indian army — those who had helped to liberate her land of birth. She wanted to meet Prayag, do something special for him, thank him and through him thank the entire Indian army.

She walked for more than half a kilometre, braving the winter chill of January 1972, to meet Prayag. She carried a box of *gur sandesh*, a Bengali sweet, neatly wrapped in a bright red cloth. She had prepared the sweets herself — as if someone else's touch would have taken away the purity and love.

It was cold outside, so cold that not many dared to venture out. In another hour all shops would close.

Sitting on a reclining chair made of cane, she waited for more than an hour and a half. Perhaps Prayag's train was delayed. There was no way to find out the revised time of arrival. It was getting colder, and could be felt to the bones through the window that Prayag's nephew, Ravi, was refusing to shut.

Damyanti shivered, but was adamant that she would only go home after meeting Prayag. But Mrs Srivastav, Ravi's mother, feared that a long exposure to cold especially during the walk home could be detrimental to her health. She insisted that Damyanti went home and promised to get Prayag to meet her the next morning. She decided to leave only after extracting two promises from Mrs Srivastav — one, that no one would eat the sweets until Ravi's uncle had eaten to his heart's content, and second, he would be brought to meet her the next morning, very early in the morning.

Soumen, who had accompanied his grandmother Damyanti and was standing next to his friend Ravi by the window, was beckoned and asked to walk her back home. In slow and steady steps, holding her grandson's hand, she walked towards her home. A few steps into the walk, she looked back, smiled at Ravi, and shouted, 'Come tomorrow evening to have *gur sandesh*. Get all your friends with you, Satwinder, Riyaz, and Bhola.'

Ravi, five years old, was not able to understand the fuss around his uncle coming home. He was also not able to understand why those sweets had to wait for his uncle. For him this visit was like the ones in the past, where his uncle would not only keep his promise of getting all the gifts that he had asked for but also get a few more to surprise him.

But, for Mrs Srivastav and Damyanti, this visit was very different. For Mrs Srivastav, her brother was coming back alive and healthy, surviving a war; and for Damyanti, Prayag was coming back as a hero, from winning the war of independence for Bangladesh.

Lieutenant Prayag's train reached Patna very late in the night.

Damyanti woke up early in the morning to prepare breakfast for him. She wanted to cook each dish herself. It was cold and heavy fog weighed the day down. The water was as cold as ice, but that didn't seem to deter her. She had left her main door open and kept checking to see if Prayag had arrived.

As promised, Mrs Srivastav ensured that Prayag left for her house by 9 am. Holding the finger of his uncle, Ravi ran to keep pace with his wide steps.

'*Kaki*, do you have some more *sandesh*?' Prayag spoke loudly and with deep laughter as he entered the gate, a few metres away from the main door of the house. Damyanti rushed out on hearing his voice. He bowed down and touched her feet. She put her hand on his head to bless him and hugged him. As tears rolled down her cheeks, she kept uttering soft thankyous. Before he could ask her the reason for her saying thank you so many times, Gautam came out and the two got into a discussion.

Prayag did not understand that in thanking him Damyanti was thanking the entire Indian army and the brave Mrs Indira Gandhi for whom she had developed immense respect.

The breakfast was an elaborate spread and she insisted Prayag take multiple servings of each dish. She had many questions on the state of Bangladesh —, refugees, military operations and the overall destruction. She was particularly excited to hear about the battles the Pakistan army lost and saddened to hear about refugees and the destruction of national assets.

Also present for breakfast was Daljit, Paramjit's youngest son, who visited her often and she had grown fond of. She loved Daljit as one of her own. Aware that he was home for a few days from his college in Chandigarh, she also invited him for breakfast. Prayag shared several stories of bravery, loyalty, and courage; and Daljit listened to them with rapt attention and admiration.

'*Bua*, I have decided,' Daljit spoke as soon as Damyanti re-entered the room. She looked puzzled, a little taken aback by the suddenness of the statement. 'I have decided to join the Indian Army.'

'Who will be the captain of the Indian hockey team then?' she laughed.

'I'm serious. I want to join the army and fight for my country like Prayag *bhaiya*.'

After her sons Soumitro and Sumanta and niece Sahana had moved out for higher studies, Daljit had filled the vacuum in her life. She had seen him grow from a small child to a teenage adult. Damyanti found him naïve and susceptible to the influence of others. 'Ma, may his dream come true. Please make him strong and bless him with a life filled with happiness,' she kept repeating in her mind.

Daljit went back to college and to a Punjab that was changing. The seed of the divide between Hindus and Sikhs was sown a few years ago with the division of the state into Punjab, Haryana, and Himachal. Now things had begun to take an ominous turn.

Little did Prayag know that morning that his next meeting with Daljit would be in the most unfortunate situation. Daljit, who was so inspired by Prayag, would become a victim of circumstances and eventually be one of the many setbacks Damyanti would encounter.

***

The anxiety and anguish that had kept Damyanti occupied in the last decade ended with Bangladesh gaining independence. Her sons and niece were well settled in their careers and living outside Patna. She had retired from her job as professor and doctor at the Patna Medical College and spent only a couple of hours in the mornings and evenings attending to patients in her community clinic. Gradually, her world moved to her grandson Soumen and his friends.

Since Soumen's parents were posted in two different rural locations at the time of his birth, he was being raised at his grandmother's house. His grandparents had become so fond of him that his parents Sumanta and Sarika had decided to let him stay on even after they were posted together.

Every evening, after playing for a couple of hours, Soumen's friends came over to the house to some of the tastiest snacks cooked under the supervision of Damyanti. And as they sat around her, chatting and playing, they decided the menu for the next day. Preparing those evening snacks had become an integral part of her life and she looked forward to it. She loved pampering each one of them. She saw her own childhood in them. She wished the children grew up loving each other and lived a long life as friends; something that she had looked forward to for herself but could not experience. She wished for them all that fate had denied her and through them wanted to live the life she could not.

Bhola, Satwinder, Riyaz, Ravi, and Madhav were with Soumen everyday. Bhola was the son of Babloo Yadav, a small-time lawyer and a budding politician. Satwinder was Paramjit's grandson. Riyaz was the son of Zafar Iqbal, a professor in Patna University, and Rehana, a teacher in a government school. Ravi's father, Amitabh Srivastav, was an engineer with the Electricity Board, and his mother was a homemaker. Madhav's father, Lallan Paswan, was working as a security guard at Paramjit's house and used to stay in a small one-room quarter there. These kids had become Damyanti's world.

Her intense emotional involvement in the East Bengal crisis had made her a keen observer of the changing landscape of Indian politics. The skies had become shadowed by darkness in the three years after the war, and nowhere was it more visible than in Patna. A very strong advocate of people's rights and independence of judiciary, Gautam and she had been worried over the past few incidents.

In August 1971, the Parliament passed the 24th Amendment to the Constitution. This Act gave the Parliament the power to dilute fundamental rights through amendments to the Constitution. In December 1971, the Parliament passed the 26th Amendment abolishing the Privy Purse. This was again done to nullify a Supreme Court ruling in favour of the princely states.

Damyanti was not only worried that these Acts were against the foundation of the Constitution and could be used by the Parliamentarians for their own gains but also in the way they were brought in. She saw the Acts as blatant misuse of power and an attack on the judiciary.

Towards the end of 1972, a frustrated Damyanti suggested that Gautam form a body called 'Forum for Information and Responsible Social Transformation' (FIRST) along with two retired colleagues and two junior lecturers. The objective was to bring forth honest inputs and analyses to the government. The inputs the forum submitted through letters to the government and articles in newspapers and magazines were largely academic in nature, seldom confrontational.

The Congress always took pride in having a democratic structure. Based on individual merit and capability, a leader from *taluk* could grow to be a national leader. A leader was never imposed on the members of the party and was always democratically elected. After the split of Congress in 1969, Mrs Gandhi put people close to her in all important positions.

On October 2, 1972, Gautam wrote an article in *The Indian Nation* urging leaders of the Congress to introspect, keeping in mind the teachings of Gandhi. He advised them to go back to the democratic structure of the party and not allow power to be concentrated to a few.

His article was as if an old headmaster was gently telling an errant pupil the greatness of his ancestors, the reputation of his family, and the importance of following their footsteps and protecting the family glory. Not many noticed that newspaper article.

On the eve of Republic Day in 1973, the Congress sponsored an advertorial and a write-up in various dailies. It spoke about constant growth in economy since independence, the total power output growing ten-fold in twenty years, development of villages, Green Revolution, and setting up of many institutes in the field of engineering, medicine, sciences and higher education.

The members of FIRST discussed all the points in their next meeting. Though Gautam had requested the members to just write a letter to the government to make it aware of the facts and not a newspaper article in response, overzealous junior members ended up publishing an article. The article carried names of three senior members, including Gautam. It countered almost all the points of the advertorial.

The article dismissed the growth figures. It made a strong case that while at an overall level these were correct they masked the regional variations and imbalances. The article was scathing in its comments on failure to increase basic education. It was also critical of the lack of initiatives in alleviating poverty.

'Gautam, what a hard-hitting article?' Damyanti said, folding the newspaper.

'Which article, Daam?'

'Come on, as if you have written many articles this week.'

Gautam snatched the newspaper from his wife and flipped through the pages. He read the piece and spoke with his head buried in his hands, 'Daam, I had not wanted this to come out. We should have written to the government.' And then with a sigh, he said, 'Anyway, not many will read this.'

He was wrong. The article had appeared next to the editorial and was read by many. Gautam was one of the most respected professors in Patna University and his association with FIRST added a lot of credibility to the forum. In the next one day, the total membership of FIRST grew to around hundred, and in the next one week to around two thousand.

'Daam, I'm surprised to see the public reaction and the way people have been joining FIRST, especially students from Patna University.'

'It's a nicely written article, factually correct and an eye opener.'

'It's not the article alone. There is simmering anger in the people, disillusionment with the political system. I had not realized the extent of the anger. The article has become a unifying force, and FIRST a hope for many. Daam, if this anger continues, it will...'

As days progressed, the overall condition in the country became worse with rising inflation, unemployment, and lack of essential commodities. The movement of students in Bihar intensified and began extending outside. A number of student unions affiliated to various political parties merged to form the Chhatra Sangharsh Samiti, CSS. In due course, FIRST merged with CSS.

While most people blamed Mrs Gandhi and her party for corruption and misrule, Damyanti remained resolute in her faith in her. In her view, Mrs Gandhi could do no wrong.

She still carried in her heart the hurt of the partition. She hated the people responsible for the division and carnage. And just when she was beginning to reconcile with her hurtful and gory past, the East Pakistan crisis emerged. Every time she read or heard about the inhuman treatment of her fellow Bengalis across the border, she had wept. The vile Pakistani army men did not even spare her young Bashir.

The global powers, always the first to speak on issues of human rights violation, turned a blind eye to carnage of such magnitude — in her view not very different from the persecution of Jews by the Nazis. It was when she had lost all hope that Mrs Gandhi emerged — the diminutive but strong lady.

Mrs Gandhi stood against the powerful Americans to fight for justice. It was the brave Indian and Bengali soldiers who won the war against the Pakistani army, but braver was the Iron Lady who decided to go to war against world opinion. In her eyes, the lady who had corrected one of the biggest wrongs in history could do no wrong. She blamed people around Mrs Gandhi for all the misdeeds.

The protests against the government became more intense and led Jay Prakash Narayan to start a movement against it. JP called for total revolution, demanded the dissolution of the Vidhan Sabha, and urged students to boycott classes for a year to focus on educating people about failure in governance, corruption, black marketing, and hoarding.

In due course, the Bihar movement became a national movement, paralysing Bihar and subsequently the entire country.

On June 12, 1975, Justice Jagmohan Lal Sinha, a judge in Allahabad High Court, originally from Bihar, ruled in favour of Raj Narain in a case against Mrs Gandhi. She was accused of using government machinery in her election campaign. Her election was declared null and she ceased to be a member of the Lok Sabha. She was barred from contesting elections for the next six years. On the same day, election results in Gujarat declared the defeat of Congress to Janata Morcha, a combination of several political parties.

On June 25, JP held a rally in Delhi urging police and government officers to refuse taking orders from the prime minister since she had lost the moral right to govern. Mrs Gandhi viewed this an as act to incite rebellion against her.

Damyanti woke up the next morning amidst commotion outside. She had returned late from the hospital the night before. Gautam was admitted in PMCH a week back. He was detected to have had a mild heart stroke and was only released after the doctors were sure that he was out of danger. Tired and weak, Gautam was still asleep.

'Ramu, what's the noise about?' she asked.

Ramu went out and came back running in ten minutes. '*Didi*, people are saying that Jay Prakash Babu has been arrested. Many other leaders have been arrested too. There is a large crowd outside his house.'

'But was JP *babu* not in Delhi yesterday?' she said, not expecting an answer.

'Yes, *didi*. I think he was arrested there.'

Damyanti rushed and switched on the radio as the clock struck eight. In a sombre voice, someone was reading the proclamation of Emergency. Fakhruddin Ali Ahmed, President of India, had signed the decree under Prime Minister's Rule a day before. The reason cited was threat to national security; a poor economy with oil crisis, made worse by internal situation; and the government paralysed with continuous strikes and protests. She rushed to get the newspaper, only to realise that the hawker had not delivered it.

The newspaper was not published that morning and many mornings thereafter because of power blackouts. Press censorship was imposed nationwide. In the next few days, several opposition leaders, many of whom were from Jan Sangh, were arrested.

Gautam had become weak and was not keeping well. Aghast at the arrogance of the government and arrests of so many senior leaders, he often complained to Damyanti, but her faith in Mrs Gandhi remained intact.

She believed that opposition parties had paralysed the government with frequent protests and their demand for an overall resignation of MLAs and MPs was not fair. She was confident that Mrs Gandhi would lift the Emergency in a few months, if not weeks, and would release the leaders soon. She thought that the imposition of Emergency was Mrs Gandhi's way of sending a message to the Opposition.

Paramjit and Daljit came to see Gautam the next day. Damyanti felt that Daljit looked disturbed and lost. She called for Gautam, who was lying in the adjacent room. Gautam walked inside. Before she could begin speaking to him, she heard Ramu shout, '*Didi*.' She turned towards the main door. Ramu came running inside, fear written all over him.

'*Didi*, there are policemen outside…asking for our house.'

'Are you sure? How many are there? They could be Gautam's students or friends of Soumitro or Sumanta.'

No, *didi*...'

Before Ramu could finish his sentence, there were rapid knocks on the door, as if someone was hitting with a stick. The door was not bolted, and in walked five policemen, three in uniform and two plainclothes.

'Professor Gautam?' the policeman in plainclothes asked.

Gautam nodded his head, bewildered at their sudden presence.

'Sir, you are under arrest.'

Paramjit got up, stood between the officer and Gautam, and roared, 'Professor *saheb* is not going anywhere. If any of you touch him the entire neighbourhood will chase you to your police station. Go away.'

'Sir, you are interfering with the law.'

Damyanti asked the officer, gaining back her composure after the initial shock, 'May I see the arrest warrant?'

'No, Madam. Professor *saheb* is being arrested under MISA.'

MISA, the Maintenance of Internal Security Act, was a law passed by Parliament in 1971 that gave the law enforcement agencies extensive power. It allowed indefinite preventive detention without any arrest warrant. It was immune from any judicial review, even though it was against the fundamentals of the Constitution.

'And, may I ask the reason for this arrest?'

'Madam, Sir has been termed as an enemy of the state. He has written articles inciting public against an elected government.'

'Do you even realise what you are saying, officer. Gautam, an enemy of the state? Do you know that he has been a freedom fighter, has never vied for political office though many leaders insisted that he join them?' Damyanti was shaking with anger.

'Daam, they are just following orders. There is no point shouting at them. Officer, please give me five minutes and I will leave with you,' Gautam spoke, getting up from his seat. He walked inside, took his walking stick and a few medicines. He was gone in fifteen minutes, leaving the room in a state of shock.

***

It had been more than two hours since the sun had set. She tried making a few frantic phone calls, but could not reach anyone. She called her son and daughter-in-law, but was told that they had gone to Lucknow. Paramjit left late in the night, leaving Daljit with her. Helpless, she retired to her room, but could hardly sleep. She woke up at 4 a.m. and found Daljit already awake. It was agreed that both of them would go to the secretariat to request the home secretary for his intervention. She was aware that Mr. Sharma, the home secretary, had a lot of respect for Gautam and her. And if he was not able to help, she would seek support from Mr. Lele, the chief secretary. Mr. Lele's son, an IPS officer of Assam cadre, had been Gautam's student.

Paramjit was at her house by 8. But, afraid that he may lose his temper in front of the officers, she requested him to stay back. Along with Daljit, Damyanti reached the Secretariat by 8:30 a.m., knowing well that people would come to work only after 10 am. She was surprised to see most of the staff in office by 9:15. The imposition of Emergency had brought back discipline in workplaces; even trains were running on time.

She sat on a small bench outside the office of the home secretary while Daljit stood, leaning against the opposite wall. After waiting for an hour, she saw Mr. Sharma walk towards his room. She got up from the bench, smiled at him, and for a fleeting moment their eyes met. He was quick to look the other way and started a conversation with the man walking beside him. She understood she had lost her case. His secretary went inside thrice to inform him that she was waiting, but he came back every time to tell her that his boss was busy and might not be able to meet that day.

Frustrated after waiting for three hours, she walked towards the office of the chief secretary. She was informed that he was in a meeting and would only meet with prior appointment. Angered by the insensitivity of everyone that she had come across, she refused to leave without meeting him. His personal assistant went in to inform him and she was ushered inside in fifteen minutes.

The chief secretary listened to her patiently but feigned ignorance about the arrest. His promises to look into the issue sounded hollow.

Damyanti came out of the room dejected. For some reason, she felt that the chief secretary wanted to help her but was powerless. Her hope of getting senior officers to get Gautam released fell. She wanted to meet him, spend some time with him, talk to him, and give him medicines he had forgotten to take. No one could tell her the place of his detention or take her there. Leaning against Daljit, she walked with slow and defeated steps.

The reaction of the officers came as a rude jolt to her. The behaviour of the officers who had come to arrest Gautam could have been an aberration, but the indifference of such senior officers was indicative of a larger failure in the system. Scared, depressed, and dejected, she blamed everyone but Mrs Gandhi.

Damyanti reached her home to find a group of young

men shouting slogans. The news of Prof. Gautam Roy's arrest had spread like wildfire at the university. A large procession was held on campus and a group of students decided to meet her to express their solidarity. She called them home and offered tea. There was fire in the eyes of the students, the intensity of which could burn any government.

Any other time, she would not have been as worried about Gautam. Not that he had not been to jail earlier, but his health had not been as bad. Damyanti felt like pleading those responsible for his arrest, telling them that her husband was sick and in no ways capable of inflicting damage on any government. She wanted to go to Delhi and plead with Mrs Gandhi for his release. But, people said that the actual power lay with her son and his group of friends, most of them young and inexperienced, some brash and arrogant.

Gautam was put in Beur Central Jail in Patna. Clandestinely, with the help of a friend of Soumitro, who was posted as Development Commissioner in Patna, she went to meet him. She picked a few books, extra stock of medicines, a few pairs of *dhoti* and *kurta*, and two bed sheets. She met him in the jailor's office. Gautam looked weaker than when he had left home. If one night could do this to him, she worried what a longer tenure would lead to. The couple spent half an hour in the room, holding hands and talking. She was struggling to hold her tears, but was determined not to show her weakness. As soon as she came out of the jail, she burst into tears.

In a week, Gautam was shifted to Bangalore Jail. Damyanti was devastated. In the last twenty-nine years, she had never felt as helpless. Twenty-nine years ago, standing in front of Gautam's mother who had lost her daughter in the most inhuman manner, amidst sounds of wails and cries of loved ones, and dead bodies and blood lying everywhere, she had felt as helpless. Age had withered away her strength. Also, unlike Noakhali, where Gautam was beside her, she was left all alone.

The realization that she had to fight this battle alone began to give her strength. She needed to meet someone powerful in Delhi, if required, Mrs Gandhi herself. The Emergency was opposed by almost all political parties, including the Communist Party of India (Marxist). However, the Communist Party of India (CPI) supported the imposition of Emergency and she decided to take their help to reach out to the office of Mrs Gandhi. Digging into her old contacts of the Communist Party in Calcutta and some that Gautam and she had developed relations with in Patna, she got a senior leader to speak to the office of Mrs Gandhi. The officer spoke to someone close to Sanjay Gandhi and she was asked to meet a young woman, supposedly a part of his inner circle, one with considerable influence. She took a train to Delhi, and, after waiting for three days, was granted an audience with the woman.

Dressed in a crisp *salwar kameez*, with sunglasses firmly perched on her head, and surrounded by young men waiting for her instructions, the woman was seated in a large, clean, decorated room. Damyanti was ushered in to meet her. She looked like a woman in hurry.

'Yes,' she said, while signing some papers.

Damyanti explained to her the reason for being there and made an impassioned plea for her husband. She spoke of his being a freedom fighter and a professor of great repute and standing, how he had never aligned himself to any political party in spite of several invitations, and his recent heart attack and failing health.

The woman took out a folder and read for some time before she spoke.

'Everyone born before independence claims to be a freedom fighter. Your husband is a founder of FIRST, now a part of Chhatra Sangharsh Samiti. He is held responsible for working against the government and has been charged with inciting people through his articles.'

Suppressing her anger, Damyanti said, 'But those articles were constructive articles for the society. In fact, he had no role in the other articles. FIRST was founded for academia and not for any agitation. He has nothing to do with the student agitations. His health doesn't permit him to be outside of home for a long time.'

'We are aware that his arrest led to a large procession

in Patna University. I am sorry, but we have also been told that there was a closed-door meeting between you and the students at your place the same day and several government officers are involved in trafficking messages from him to the people who are underground. You may not like to hear this, but the needle of suspicion points to you as well.' There was arrogance and contempt in every sentence that the woman uttered.

'So, why don't you arrest me?'

The woman was taken aback at this sudden defiance.

Damyanti got up from her seat, thanked the woman for the meeting, and walked towards the door. She had barely taken a few steps when she turned and came back.

'Are you married?'

'No.'

'*Beta*, when you get married and have kids, please give them the right education. Give them the right upbringing to help them appreciate our history and culture, make them sensitive, and give them the knowledge to distinguish right from wrong. Believe me, you will do a service to the nation by doing so. Power is constructive only in hands that belong to sensitive minds; otherwise it is dangerous and destructive.'

There was absolute silence as she walked out of the room.

Damyanti left Delhi dejected and in despair. Not only had she lost hope of an early release for Gautam, but was also dreading the future that she could see.

Damyanti felt very lonely without Gautam and guilty that he was in jail while she was living in the comfort of her home. She had rarely been away from him in the last four decades, and whenever he had gone to Delhi for work related to Bihar government, she knew exactly when he would be back. His absence, the thought of the conditions he might be living in, uncertainty around his return, and his deteriorating health was killing her. She felt weak, very weak.

Suddenly, Damyanti was scared. Corruption was not limited to a few government departments and a few politicians and bureaucrats. The woman who spoke to her with arrogance, whose integrity was questionable and intent dubious, was representative of an ever-growing tribe. It was not the failure of a group of individuals or a particular set of processes, but of the system. There was lack of political will to counter these evils. To be in power at any cost was most important. And that is what worried her.

She also worried for Soumen and his friends. How would they be able to cope and survive an environment that was getting polluted by the day? How could they be better prepared for a tomorrow that was destined to be dark?

The journey back to Patna was laden with worry. She was worried that she might not get any news of Gautam. There were talks that the Congress would convert Parliament into a Constituent assembly and get necessary amendments to have a Presidential form of government. It was rumoured that the Emergency might not be lifted for eight years and the prisoners would be kept in jails till then. People were so terrified that she feared she might not get any help from friends and colleagues. Feeling weak and alone, she got down at Patna Station.

Daljit and Paramjit were the first people to come and meet her. In some time, the news of Gautam being transferred to Bangalore Jail and her failed mission in Delhi spread in the neighbourhood and university. There was a stream of visitors; almost everyone that they knew in Patna came down to meet her. Her cousins from Calcutta also came down. And everyone who came spoke of having someone close in Bangalore who could meet Gautam frequently and keep a watch.

Seeing people come to meet her so openly gave her the hope that they would rise against the Emergency.

Damyanti took down the contacts of a few people in Bangalore and left for the city. It was agreed that Rakesh, son of Prof. Arvind, and a young professor at IISc, would meet Gautam on a frequent basis. He was introduced to Manohar, Assistant Commissioner of Police, and Mr. Dewan, a businessman with a lot of clout. He was told to contact them in case he faced any issues. Manohar and Mr. Dewan, courteous, sympathetic, and extremely helpful, were related to her friends from Patna.

Confident of the arrangements made, she returned to Patna.

***

After a few days of her return from Bangalore, on 15th August, Damyanti switched on her radio to the tragic news of the assassination of Sheikh Mujibur Rahman. Sheikh's entire family was wiped out by the rebel army. The only surviving members were his daughters, Sheikh Haseena and Rehana, who were in West Germany at the time of the assassination. They were flown to India under the protection of the Indian government.

For Damyanti, this brutal assassination was not merely the death of an important leader who was the hope of Bangladesh but also an omen of things to come. Partition had been unfortunate and painful, but after that things had been fine for her in Patna. The only darkness that had remained was the inhuman and partisan treatment meted to her brothers and sisters of East Bengal by Pakistanis, and the liberation of Bangladesh had successfully ended that.

Relieved that popular governments who had their nations' interest at heart governed both countries, Damyanti was confident that nothing could go wrong. And then, things began to change. All around she saw divisiveness, corruption, greed, and lack of virtues required for good governance. She knew that the imposition of Emergency and the assassination of Sheikh Mujib were not merely isolated incidents but would have long lasting effects on the respective nations.

As expected, she received a letter from Samina in a few weeks. The letter spoke of two deaths — one that she was aware of and the second that came as a deeper shock. Salim had suffered a massive heart attack on hearing about the brutal killing of Sheikh Mujib and his family and never recovered from it. He passed away in the presence of his sister and brother-in-law. On his deathbed, he remembered Bashir a lot and often spoke of his desire to meet a few people one last time — Damyanti was one of them. Holding the letter, with her head against the portrait of Ma Durga, Damyanti cried inconsolably.

The news of Salim's death came without any warning. Her last meeting with him in Calcutta had given her hope that she might be able to meet him a few more times. She wanted to say sorry to him; wanted to explain the sudden change that he had noticed in her decades ago; how she had felt helpless and torn then, and defeated later; how if only she was a few years older then she would have dealt with it differently, maybe in a more mature manner. Had she known that she would be meeting him in Calcutta, she would have prepared herself better.

The pain of Salim's passing was compounded by the knowledge that he had died unaware about what had changed her. She hated herself at that moment for not having the courage to tell him, if not for withstanding against laid out societal norms. She felt rage at the situation, on Bijoy for not standing up for his love that day, at her father for imposing a decision on Bijoy that appeared wrong then but criminal now, and at everyone who held religion more important than human bonds.

But, Salim had spoken to her in Calcutta as if he didn't hold anything against her, as if he understood her compulsions without knowing the specifics. But that was Salim, always indulgent towards her.

In November, JP was released due to failing health. He was diagnosed with failure of both kidneys and put on dialysis for life.

The outcome of the implementation of the 20-point program introduced by Mrs Gandhi had been good. Intelligence provided to Mrs Gandhi spoke of her popularity among common people and their confidence in her. On hearing the sentiment, the idea of holding an election started germinating in her mind. The government began to release political leaders, but ordinary members were still in jail. With a large number of members of political parties in jail, there were very few people available to do ground work.

In the first week of September, Damyanti received a

telegram from Bangalore. Telegrams were mostly sent to convey sad news and hence she opened it with a lot of anxiety. Her happiness knew no bounds when she read it. The government had agreed to release Gautam, and Rakesh would accompany him to Patna.

In a couple of days, she received another telegram conveying the date of arrival. The news was immediately relayed to Sarika and Sumanta, her daughter-in-law and younger son.

Damyanti's house had been in gloom for a long time. The news of Gautam's release and impending return brought cheer and happiness. The joy extended to the entire neighbourhood and friends.

Gautam's train was to reach Patna station at 1 pm. There was a feast waiting for him. Damyanti had herself cooked *hilsa* fish and *aalo-posto*, his favourite. A large bowl of butter chicken, another favourite, was sent from Paramjit's house. Ramu had bought an assortment of Bengali sweets and refused to accept money for it. The train reached before the scheduled arrival time. She was there to receive him.

Gautam came out of the train in very slow steps. He looked weak and tired. He had often complained of chest pain in jail but was never provided medical attention. He was coughing a lot. She had met him several months back and had noticed him coughing intermittently but dismissed it as a throat infection. Now, the intensity of coughing was dangerously high. In six months, he looked like a shadow of what he was.

Paramjit ran towards him and hugged him while she stood staring at him.

Gautam needed immediate medical attention. She took him to Patna Medical College the next day. He was diagnosed with tuberculosis, high blood sugar, and problems in the heart. Though a surgery was required immediately, other complications made it near impossible. The best doctors of Patna Medical College were attending to his case and looked in a state of despair.

Sarika and Sumanta reached Patna after a few days. Damyanti's helplessness kept growing; her anxiety had got the better of her. Only God could save Gautam. She wanted to visit Kalighat temple in Calcutta, beg Ma Kali to save his life. Many decades ago, when Gautam had fallen sick and doctors were not able to cure him, she had taken refuge at the feet of Ma Kali there. She had begged Ma for help and Ma had not disappointed her. It seemed like yesterday. She decided to go to Calcutta the next day with Sumanta, leaving Sarika to take care of Gautam. She went to bed that night with the confidence that Ma Kali would cure Gautam once she prayed at the temple.

She woke up early next morning. Gautam, who normally got up early, before his wife, was still in bed. He must be very tired, she thought, and left him to sleep. An hour later, she heard Sumanta scream. She rushed towards the room in panic.

'*Maa, Baba* is not responding. *Maa…*'

She ran towards Gautam and examined him closely. The wife in her had a ray of hope that he would survive, but the doctor in her knew that he was no more. Gautam had passed away in his sleep.

'Gautam was a saint, away from all that he was accused of. He was a true patriot and a socialist. Your father could have lived longer. The last one year took away ten years of his life. I'll never forgive…' Her voice trailed as she spoke to Sumanta. This was the first time she came close to blaming Mrs Gandhi.

Mrs Gandhi, with all the intelligence to differentiate right from wrong and the power to prevent wrong, had allowed this to happen.

On the insistence of the students of Patna University, Gautam's body was taken in a small procession to the banks of the Ganga for cremation. Gradually, the procession became bigger, and though not permitted during Emergency, the authorities turned a blind eye. The cremation was also attended by a few bureaucrats of the state government, some of who had been his students.

On January 18, 1977, Mrs Gandhi announced that elections would happen in two months. JP travelled the length and breadth of the country to campaign for candidates of the Janata Party, a party he had helped form by amalgamation of various political parties. He drew more crowds than Mrs Gandhi. The bottled anger against the two years of Emergency was pouring out.

Mahamaya Prasad Sinha, a freedom fighter and erstwhile Congress leader, was the candidate of Janata Party for the Patna Lok Sabha seat. Damyanti was invited for his campaigns and she attended most meetings. Every time that she stood to speak, she was welcomed with enthusiastic slogans of 'Professor Roy *Amar Rahe*' and 'Doctor *Sahiba Zindabad*'. Her request to vote for Sinha was heard by the people present and beyond.

The election results were announced on 23rd March. Janata Party along with its allies had a comfortable two-thirds majority in the Lok Sabha. Mrs Gandhi and Sanjay Gandhi lost from their respective seats. In Bihar, Janata Party had a clean sweep, winning all 53 seats. Morarji Desai was the new Prime Minister of India.

***

After Gautam's death, Sarika came to Patna frequently to meet her mother-in-law. She was worried about her living alone and often insisted that she stayed with them in Lucknow.

'*Maa*, please come and stay with us. With *baba* gone, please don't stay in Patna alone. It will not only be difficult for you to manage but also you will feel very lonely,' Sarika pleaded during one of her visits.

'This is my home, *beta*,' Damyanti said softly. 'I had always wanted to live in Dacca and as a child foolishly thought that I will always have my friends next to me. I had an identity and immense respect in the city, largely because of our family and partly because of my profession. Some of the best memories that I have are of my childhood friends. Then fate snatched away everything from me, first friends and then Dacca.' She walked and sat beside Sarika. 'Sarika, you know that Soumen is my life. I am reliving my childhood through him. In his friends, I see my friends. I want each one of them to grow up and have deep relationships till they grow old, something that I couldn't have. And, I'm determined to work towards that.'

'But *maa*, alone in this city?'

'I am not alone, Sarika. And even if I am alone later, does it matter? This city has given me an identity. Love and respect. It continuously reminds me of Dacca. You know, *beta*, I took a lot of pride in the communal harmony that I saw in Dacca. And then, things began to change. I do not blame the people for the change, but the political leaders, their greed and intentions. Patna can never be what Dacca is, but it keeps reminding me of the old days in Dacca, the same sense of communal harmony and security. Patna to me is what Dacca could not be, what Dacca should have been. It accepted me with open arms and gave me security in my weakest phase. How can I leave this place?'

'But *Maa*, times are changing. Increasingly, society is experiencing more fissures amongst people. How will you manage?'

'I could not several decades back. I failed, became weak and allowed circumstances and situations to over-power me. I fled, maybe I should not have. Or, maybe that was the right thing to do. But the point is that I did not fight. But not now, *beta*. Should such a situation arise, I am determined to fight back. I do not know what the future holds for me, but I know that I will not allow myself to be weak.'

Damyanti wiped away tears from her eyes. 'Sarika, I want Soumen to have all that I missed in my life. All. I am being selfish. I want him to experience bonds of friend-ship that I could not. I want him to be attached to this city like I am to Dacca, but unlike me enjoy that attachment throughout his life. Through him, I want to live a life that I could not.'

Sarika hugged her *maa as* tears refused to stop from their eyes. The two women remained locked in embrace.

What Damyanti did not tell her daughter-in-law was the guilt of Gautam's death that she was living with. At each stage in life, Gautam had made sacrifices for her. She was always pampered; her wishes always paid heed to. The last two years had been torturous for him, mentally and physically, full of hardships, while she had led a life with physical comforts in Patna. If it was one of the two who had to go through this, the one who should have died, it should have been her. She did not want to live a life of comfort at Sumanta's place, not without Gautam, not after what he had gone through.

Little did Damyanti know that the worst was yet to come.

PART III

Nadir Kul nai, kinar nai re
Ami kon kul hote, kon kule jabo?
Kahare shudhai re, nadir kul nai, kinar nai re....

The river has no shore , no bank
From which coast I'll sail to which, whom do I ask?
The river has no shore, no bank …

Chapter 11

Had it not been for her grandson Soumen and his friends, the sorrow of Gautam's death would have killed Damyanti. Lonely, forlorn, and melancholic, she diverted her attention and time to the kids.

Soumen and his friends were growing up very fast. That the last two years had been tough for *Doctor Dadi* was not hidden from them, and hence their visits to her house had been less frequent. The change in government brought back overall stability. Soon, the routine was restored with the kids assembling in her house every evening to sumptuous snacks and unstoppable showers of love.

In order to be with the kids in the evening, Damyanti altered her time of consultation at the clinic. She ensured that she had discussions with each one of them every evening. She probed them on their likes, fears, interests, problems, etc. If she noticed that a kid was tense, she spoke to him about his problems and made those look easy and trivial. The kids always left their tensions behind when they walked out of *Doctor Dadi's* house.

Often, incidents reminded her of her childhood. She loved such journeys to the time that was left behind in the distant past and yet appeared so recent.

Soumen was intelligent, brilliant in Maths and Science, and was always ranked among the top two of his class. He was growing to be an avid quizzer and debater. He was gentle, pleasant, compassionate and affable, the binding glue that brought the friends together, and his grandmother's pride.

Ravi was a year older than Soumen but in the same class as him. He was good in studies and very hard working. His family wanted him to be an IAS officer. Gradually, that became his ambition in life.

Satwinder, Paramjit's grandson, was a year younger to Soumen. He had great acumen for machines and mechanical devices and often talked about running his family's automobile garage. He loved eating and his *Doctor Dadi* loved feeding him. He was full of life and laughter.

Riyaz was in the same class as Ravi and Soumen. Soumen and he were very close and often studied together at each other's house. Usually calm, he rarely got into an argument.

Riyaz had a sister, Saira, three years younger — a beautiful child, lovely and adorable, loved by the entire neighbourhood and most by Damyanti. Saira enjoyed all the attention from her *Doctor Dadi*.

Bhola was two years older than Soumen and one-year senior in class. His father, Babloo Yadav, had left his legal practice and moved full time into politics. He was a student at the local government school, good in studies and sports. He was strong and brave, always willing to fight for his friends.

Madhav, son of Lallan Paswan, was two years younger to Soumen. Damyanti helped Madhav with his studies, and after everyone left for their homes in the evening, he stayed back for a couple of hours to study. He studied in a small school, where the quality of teaching was not very good. The classes left him with lots of unanswered questions. What began as small sessions to clarify these doubts gradually got converted to full-fledged classes for Damyanti.

In due course, Babban, Lallan's nephew, became a part of the group. His father was a farm labourer in Punjab. Lallan had bought a small piece of land that fell between large tracts of land of the village strongman Bhagwan Yadav. Bhagwan had set his eyes on that piece of land and Babban's mother's constant refusal to give that away often led to bitter argument. Babban was away when Bhagwan's goons raped his mother and burnt the house, resulting in the tragic death of his mother and sister. Lallan brought him to Patna under Damyanti's shelter.

In the boys, she saw her friends, some dead by then. In Soumen, she saw Salim — intelligent, compassionate, caring, and always in control. Ravi was her Tapan — diligent, hardworking, and loyal. Madhav was Arup, sensitive to the core. Bhola was her Manas, adept in the ways of the world. The kids were her world, her reason for existence, her vehicle to unfulfilled dreams.

If Daljit had been a girl, he would have been Parineeta — emotional and confused, easily swayed by passions. He had not been to Patna for more than two years. No one knew what he was doing in faraway Punjab.

The Green Revolution brought in prosperity to Punjab and large-scale unemployment. The state was in the grip of vices like liquor, drugs, and adultery. Influenced by his professors, Daljit began working towards educating young men in villages about the ill effects of these vices and was gradually drawn into a larger network of preachers and activists. He joined Damdami Taksal and came in contact with Bhindranwale's men. Sant Bhindranwale, initially only a preacher, was rumoured to have been positioned as an opposition to the Akalis by the Congress. With time, Bhindranwale became a secessionist demanding a separate country for the Sikhs. Many of his followers became militants. Daljit, though not a militant, could not avoid being part of the group since many of them were his friends from Damdami Taksal. By the time he realized what he had gotten into, he was trapped.

Mrs Gandhi came back to power after the elections in 1980. The Janata experiment failed miserably.

Soumen and Madhav were preparing for IIT. Damyanti had bought them complete sets of books from Agrawal Classes to train and practice. Riyaz was preparing for admission to medical colleges. Ravi and Bhola wanted to study in Delhi University and prepare for Indian Civil Services. Satwinder was planning to go to Canada for his studies.

To everyone's surprise, Babban began showing immense potential as a cricketer. On Soumen's request, Damyanti bought him a complete cricket set and spoke to a local club, requesting them to train him. As his game improved, she spoke to the president of the Patna Cricket Association. Babban did not disappoint his *Dadi*. He was selected for the junior team of the Patna district, then state, and finally, to the utter delight of his friends and *Dadi*, in the fifteen-member Under-17 Team India.

The Under-17 Indian team was scheduled to travel to Australia. It was going to be Babban's first overseas travel. The trip was to take place in December. Not having met his father for more than a year, Babban wanted to meet him before leaving for Australia. His father was working near Amritsar. Lallan accompanied him to Amritsar during the *Durga Puja* vacations. They took a train to Amritsar and then a bus there on October 5, 1983, to the village where Babban's father was.

Punjab was experiencing an increase in militancy, with rampant killing of innocents. A group of young men close to Daljit was planning to attack buses on the highway the day Lallan and Babban left Amritsar. Daljit's friends lied to him, saying they would only loot a few rich men and not harm anyone. Reluctantly, he agreed to accompany them.

It was 1 pm and a bright sun shone on an otherwise cold day. Lallan's bus slowed down near a sharp bend on the highway. Suddenly, four people came in front of the bus, forcing the driver to apply the brakes. Leaving Daljit and one more person outside, ten men with weapons got in. Daljit was facing away from the bus a little distance away. The men carefully segregated Hindus, people not wearing turbans, and asked them to step out. All of them were asked to kneel, facing away from the bus. Several bullets were fired. Daljit turned, hearing the sound.

As he turned and saw his friends shoot the kneeling men, he heard two distinct voices shout, 'Tinu *Beta*', 'Daljit *Bhaiya*'. He was fondly called Tinu by his family. He ran towards the men, had brief eye contact with Lallan, before the latter collapsed. Lallan and Babban lay dead in a pool of blood. Daljit fainted next to their bodies.

Next morning, Damyanti read about the death of the bus passengers in the newspaper. In the list of dead was the name 'Babban Paswan'. With the newspaper in hand, she fell to the ground, unconscious. She was released from the hospital after three days — sad, devastated and bitter.

The news of Babban's death caused a brutal interruption to a beautiful dream that Damyanti had begun to see.

She had often visualized her kids as young men, busy with their careers in different parts of the country, returning to Patna and to her every year during *Durga Puja* and summer vacations. She was sure nothing could go wrong and that her kids would prosper in her love and grow up as fine men. Suddenly, the youngest of the boys was killed for no fault of his. She felt frightened, and like a lioness wanted to protect her flock. With her head pressed against the feet of Ma Durga, she kept requesting, 'Ma, no more. Please, no more.'

The spate of killings increased in the next few months. Bhindranwale and his followers, who were operating from the Golden Temple, gradually filled it with powerful arms and ammunition.

In June 1984, the Indian Army entered the Golden Temple to evict Bhindranwale and his men. Major Prayag, Ravi's uncle, an officer of the Kumaon Regiment at that time, was also a part of the operation.

Daljit was inside the Golden Temple with his friends, many of who had turned into militants. Holed in a corner behind a pillar on the hostel side, he was devastated. The Golden Temple, where a mere visit gave him the feeling of eternal peace, was witnessing the ugliest form of violence. When the first few bullets were fired, he had hoped reason would prevail. But the firing only increased and he soon saw tanks moving in. Anguished, old memories came to his mind — the endless love of his mother, family and friends. And then, Lallan and Babban, kneeling along with others, with bullets in their bodies. Strangely, this and Damyanti *bua's* image kept alternating in his mind.

His string of thoughts was broken with the sound of rushed footsteps and someone shouting 'run'. Major Prayag and his troops had entered from the hostel complex side in the south. He got up, came out from behind the pillar and was about to run inside. His friends had already run some distance. He heard a loud 'no', turned his head slightly, his eyes met that of Major Prayag.

Major Prayag was trying to tell his men not to shoot, but by then a number of bullets had already pierced his body. He shouted, '*bhaiya*' and collapsed. In the deafening sound of bullets, only Prayag heard '*bhaiya*'. Prayag wanted to tend to him, but with firing all around, he jumped over Daljit's body and hid behind another pillar, only to proceed further.

Damyanti had a bad dream that night. She saw Daljit, crying, his shirt soaked in blood. '*Bua*, I want to study further. Help me. I want to…' But the last part of the sentence was drowned out in the loud beating of drums, as if a large group of people were playing *dhak* in front of Ma Durga. She woke up with a start and could not sleep the rest of the night.

One evening, a few months after Operation Bluestar, Damyanti had an unexpected visitor in Major Prayag. He had come to meet his sister and decided to visit Damyanti, alone and unannounced. Softly, he broke the news of Daljit's death. Shocked, holding his hand in grief, she cried bitterly. Her tears refused to stop as she stood in front of the portrait of Ma Durga after Prayag left.

Standing there, she kept repeating, 'Ma, how could you?'

***

The two deaths in such a short span of time left Damyanti devastated, raising several questions. How were these deaths different from the ones she had witnessed in Noakhali, where one community brutally killed people of the other?

Babban's death was in no way different from that of Radha, both innocent and young, killed by their own people. Daljit shot in an army operation on its own people? Like during the British rule?

The more she thought about it, the more she felt terrified.

India was built on the idea of all communities living together in harmony; people had chosen to be a part of this country, unlike Pakistan, which was formed on the basis of religion. Life in Patna had only strengthened her view about communities living in harmony.

If this could happen in one part of the country, what would stop it from not repeating itself in other parts? This time it was Daljit and Babban, the next time it could be Ravi or Bhola or Soumen.

Damyanti felt weak. She worried for her children, frightened that their world could get scattered the way hers had, that there could be more Daccas, many more. Nothing seemed to have changed in the last fifty years. Was she foolish to think that time would heal old wounds and help people learn from old mistakes? But when has the human race learnt from old follies? They have only become more greedy, territorial warmongers.

***

Army action at the Golden Temple hurt the religious sentiment of the Sikhs. Emotion overtook reason. Mrs Gandhi had two Sikh bodyguards in her retinue, Satwant Singh and Sub Inspector Beant Singh. Though fiercely loyal to her, the attack on the Golden Temple left them hurt and angry, emotionally affected by what they thought was sacrilege. The men, planning to take revenge, were aware that the two bodyguards were extremely vulnerable.

On October 31, 1984, Damyanti woke up very early in the morning. She had not been able to sleep well that night. There was a lot of noise outside, which only kept increasing. Worried it could be an accident or riot, she asked Ramu to go outside and check.

Ramu came back running, his speech incoherent. '*Didi*... they are saying...they are saying...Indiraji is dead.'

'Dead!'

Damyanti had seen her in the news the earlier day. Mrs Gandhi had appeared fit. She paced towards the television. There was no mention of the prime minister's death. She switched on the radio to AIR, again no mention at all. Then she tuned to BBC and heard the news — Mrs Gandhi had been shot. She sat next to the radio, alternating between stations.

At 9:20 am, Mrs Gandhi had walked out of her residence for an interview with an English actor for a documentary on her. The bodyguards on duty were Satwant Singh and Beant Singh. As she approached them, they opened fire at her. She was immediately rushed to AIIMS hospital. The ITBF police shot Beant and Satwant was taken into custody. She was operated upon. Around thirty bullets had pierced her body, seven had remained inside and the rest had passed through.

Mrs Gandhi was declared dead at 2:20 p.m. But, the news was broken to the nation only in the evening. Damyanti forgot to eat that day. When she was not in front of the TV or radio, she stood in front of the portrait of Ma Durga with hands clasped in prayer, willing to sacrifice anything in return for Mrs Gandhi's life.

She held Mrs Gandhi responsible for Gautam's death. She also held her responsible for the death of Daljit and Babban. She blamed her for not controlling militancy and letting it grow to monstrous proportions. But, eyes closed, images of her childhood and the immense tragedy that East Bengal had to suffer crossed her mind. In those days of distress, when every day newspaper headlines bore news of deaths, destruction, and the swelling number of refugees; and Bengalis in East Bengal had lost hope and pride; the diminutive lady had stood taller and braver than anyone. Mrs Gandhi had saved Dacca, her mother, the place of her ancestors. She had helped restore Iqbal's pride, avenged Bashir's death, and helped the cause that was so dear to Salim. If there was ever a leader of steel, it was she. Damyanti would remain indebted to her in this life and many more.

Damyanti had always wanted to meet Mrs Gandhi after the Bangladesh war, but the imposition of Emergency and the incidents thereafter made it impossible. She handed over some money to Ramu and sent him to the railway station to book two tickets to New Delhi. In case of any problem in the availability of tickets, he was told to barge into the room of the stationmaster and call her from there. There were no seats available on flight.

Mrs Gandhi's body was kept in Teen Murti Bhavan for people to pay their last respects. Thousands of people travelled from all over India to bid her a final goodbye. As the nation mourned, Sikh households were targeted at several places, foolishly holding the community responsible for the ghastly death.

Damyanti reached Delhi on the morning of November 2. She could barely sleep during the journey. She was received at the station by her grandnephew, Purnendu. She was ready to go to Teen Murti Bhavan in a couple of hours.

'*Dadima*, shall I get you a wreath?' Purnendu asked her.

'No. I had never expected her to die so soon. For many years, I have wanted to meet and thank her. Sadly, something or the other kept me away. I have travelled all the way not to see her dead body but to thank her before she is reduced to ashes. I do not want to carry a wreath, maybe a bunch of flowers, something she would have liked. You cannot fathom how much we owe to her…' her voice trailed as she shifted her gaze out of the window.

She stood for three hours in the long queue of people waiting to pay their respect to Mrs Gandhi. She requested the security person to allow her to stay near the body for a little longer. Standing there, looking at Mrs Gandhi's face, she burst into tears as she kept saying thank you.

As she walked towards the exit, to the surprised security personnel who had been observing, she murmured, 'End of an era.'

Chapter 12

The new government sworn in after Mrs Gandhi's death gave lots of hope to the people in its initial days. Damyanti, constantly plagued with fear and worry for her boys, would watch news with a microscopic eye, often trying to interpret long-term implications. She feared for the remaining kids and constantly prayed for their wellbeing.

On the threshold of important career decisions, the boys needed her more than ever. Unlike their parents, who had fixed views on the courses they ought to study, she listened to them patiently, discussed and debated, and limited herself to expressing opinion in a thought-provoking manner. Most of the time, the boys found her inputs more in tune with their thoughts and ambitions than the advice they received from their parents. She was trying to help each of them build their career and at the same time be prepared for setbacks, if any.

Around this time, in a landmark judgement, the Supreme Court ruled in favour of Shah Bano in a divorce settlement case. Her husband had left her for a younger woman and refused to pay her a monthly maintenance. He had agreed to pay a small, one-time amount as per the Islamic law. The verdict was projected as an encroachment on Muslim Personal Law, with a cry for its reversal. Several Muslim men took to the street in protest. In no time, these protests became a subject of national debate.

The leaders of the Congress party felt their silence would be negatively viewed by the Muslim community and impact them in the elections.

In 1986, the Parliament passed The Muslim Women (Protection of Rights on Divorce) Act nullifying the Supreme Court judgement. As per the Act, a divorced Muslim woman was entitled to maintenance only during *Iddat* or till 90 days from the date of divorce in line with the Islamic Law.

Opposition parties and women organizations accused the Congress of appeasement of the Muslim community for electoral gains. And, leading this protest was the Bhartiya Janta Party (BJP), which not only blamed the Congress for using the community as a vote bank but also for continuous disregard of the Judiciary.

In the same year, Soumen wrote his entrance for engineering, and, as expected, did exceedingly well in the IIT-JEE entrance examinations. He chose to study electrical engineering at IIT, Delhi. Riyaz took admission in AFMC to be a doctor in the army. Ravi obtained a good result in his board examinations for Standard XII and got admitted to the history honours course in Hindu College.

As the voices blaming the government increased, a verdict was issued in 1986 by the district judge in the Ram Janambhoomi Temple case to open the gates and permit Hindus to worship. In December 1949, a few Hindu nationalists broke into the mosque and placed idols of Lord Ram inside. The Hindus believed there was a temple in Ayodhya, at the birthplace of Lord Ram, which had been demolished by Mughal Emperor Babur to build a mosque. Hindu and Muslim bodies filed court cases laying separate claims on the site. The gates remained locked. The land was declared to be under dispute, but Hindu priests were allowed to enter and perform daily worship.

People felt the verdict was a ploy of the Congress to bring back the Hindus who seemed to be getting disillusioned with the party.

***

Amidst all of this, Damyanti turned 75 in 1986. Although she was opposed to any grand celebration, she yielded to pressure from family members.

The developments in the last few years had left her bitter. It was not the past that she lamented upon more — death of loved ones, petty and divisive politics, and

increasing fragmentation of an already divided society —
but the future that these had begun to shape.

On her request, the celebrations were limited to family
members. Her niece Sahana happily volunteered to make
all the arrangements.

'*Pisi*, I'm planning a big surprise for you. I am planning a celebration in Europe and we will fly from Calcutta.
I'll book everyone's tickets,' Sahana had called Damyanti
excitedly.

Sahana and her husband had moved to India a few
years ago. He was responsible for the South Asian desk
in the Ministry of External Affairs and she was practicing in Safdurjang Hospital. She flew to Patna for a day
to get everyone to sign their visa applications. She helped
Damyanti sign her visa papers. That afternoon, Damyanti's glasses had disappeared mysteriously, only to reappear
miraculously in the night.

The family members decided to meet in Calcutta and
fly from there.

'Sahana, don't international flights take off in the
night?' Damyanti asked Sahana, getting into the car early
in the morning to go to Calcutta airport.

'Most of them, *Pisi*. Not all.'

'Which country are we going to, Sahana? England?'

Sahana just laughed. Damyanti hugged her and said,

'My darling, you shouldn't have spent so much. God only knows how much you are spending. You shouldn't have, sweetheart…'

'Sshh, *Pisi*. I have waited for this day for so many years. The past few years have been tough for all of us, but there has been so much that I'm grateful for. All of us feel blessed to have you in our lives. I want to enjoy every moment of this week that we spend together and recount all my happy memories with you.'

The group reached Calcutta airport in time. While they stood near the check in counter, Sahana carried all the tickets and collected boarding passes for everyone. One by one, she handed them over. Then, she walked towards Damyanti and handed her boarding pass with a smile. She stood in front of her aunt as the latter raised it to check the details.

Damyanti looked at the boarding pass, rubbed her eyes, and brought it closer. She kept gazing at it for some time and then raised her eyes to look at Sahana, who was standing with a wide smile on her face. Sahana stepped forward and hugged her. The two, holding each other tightly, were sobbing uncontrollably, overcome with emotion.

To Damyanti's utter surprise, beyond what she could have imagined, the boarding pass read 'Dhaka' and not any city in Europe.

Seated next to Sahana in the airplane, Damyanti was

lost in thoughts. The excitement of seeing Dacca after 40 years clouded her mind with old memories. She had often thought of going there, but something or the other had kept her busy. It took her some years to settle in a new place after leaving East Bengal.

'Couldn't I have gone for a few days in the last four decades? Was it actually so difficult? Did something hold me back? Do I keep justifying my decision or the lack of it to various insignificant reasons? If Sahana had not planned it, would I have ever seen Dacca again?'

Sahana saw tears rolling down the cheeks of her *Pisi*, but decided not to disturb her. Her *Pisi* stroked her hair and looked at her lovingly.

'How much would Dacca have changed? If I had known earlier, I would have written to Samina. Ma Durga, please help me meet my sister.' Damyanti's string of thoughts refused to cease. Her excitement kept growing as the flight approached Dhaka Airport.

***

The aircraft landed around noon. Damyanti looked out of the window and was happy to see that the weather was sunny and pleasant. She came closer to the window and stretched her gaze to look at the vast expanse beyond the runway. Things looked different, and yet familiar.

Damyanti got down with careful steps. As the rest of the group and people walked ahead, she stopped, knelt down, bent forward, touched the ground with her forehead and kissed it.

Sahana, who was standing beside her, extended her hand to help her get up. The two hugged each other and Damyanti spoke into Sahana's ears, 'Thank you, sweetheart. Thank you so much. Your father and I grew up here. I will take you to the places where we played in our childhood. He was very close to me, a man so calm and of such strong ideals.' After walking a few more steps, she spoke again, 'Sahana, if you had told me earlier, I would have written to Samina and requested her to be in station. I'm not sure if she is in Dacca.'

With a twinkle in her eyes, Sahana replied, 'But, *Pisi*, then how would I have surprised you?'

Sahana's husband, the first to come out, was welcomed by officials from the Indian embassy. Damyanti walked towards the exit with Soumen and Sahana beside her. There was a small group standing along the railing. Someone from that group seemed to be waving at her. Unable to identify them from distance, she tried hard to focus on their faces. The bright sun shining against her was not helping. The small contingent of three women and two handsome men began to walk towards her. One of the women was walking with the help of a stick.

Damyanti froze when her eyes fell on the woman in

the light green *sari*. With the suddenness of the situation and an abrupt halt, she lost her balance. Sahana immediately stepped up and held her tight. Before she could utter a single word, the woman in green hugged her tightly. Engulfed in emotion, both started crying.

'Paki...' Samina kept repeating, holding her friend and sister in a tight embrace. The other woman walked towards the two, dropped her stick, and took the two in her arms. Damyanti kept looking at her, not able to recognize her. 'Pari?'

The three friends held each other tightly as tears refused to stop. The rest of the group stood by, leaving them to savor the moment.

Samina, Parineeta, and Damyanti got into the car like three school kids. Salma, Samina's daughter; Razaq, her son; and Soumitro, Damyanti's elder son, had also come to the airport. Salma's husband had gone to Sylhet to escort Parineeta. Razaq's wife and Bashir's widow had stayed back at home to make arrangements.

'Samin, shall we go through the old market?' Damyanti requested.

'Sure, Paki.'

As the car went around the city, Damyanti immediately recognized most areas. There were a few that looked as if they had never existed. 'Have all cities not changed with time?' she wondered, as she gazed out of the window.

Her Dacca had changed in some ways and remained unchanged in many.

The car approached Dhaka Railway Station. The station building, majestic in bearing and witness to decades of history, reminded her of so many incidents. The building had remained unchanged, but so much had changed outside. The number of people and vehicles had multiplied. The place looked crowded, taking away the serenity that was once its attribute.

'Samin, can we please stop here for a few minutes?'

The driver did not wait for instruction from her mistress to stop the car. Seated on the back seat, Damyanti kept looking at the station with moist eyes. A young couple walked out of the main gate, laughing with abandon, surrounded by a few friends. It took her back in time to when she travelled with Gautam, her brother Arup, and Tapan during the holidays. She had always looked forward to those short train journeys and would often joke that a man's true character is revealed when he escorts a girl in a train. While Arup and Tapan laughed, Gautam's embarrassment would be evident to all. Even after they had decided to get married, not much had changed about the way Gautam would react. She loved being pampered by Gautam, the way he carried her bags, cleaned the seat before she sat, kept asking if she needed anything and ensured that she was comfortable. And every time they got down from the train at Dacca, she insisted that they have tea at the corner stall. Those last few minutes with Gautam, before they departed to their respective homes, were so precious to her.

She shifted her gaze from the main gate to the corner, looking for the tea stall. The stall was no longer there. In its place was a small eatery. She could only hope that the eatery belonged to the family of the tea stall owner. As the members of the group split, she saw the young girl bid adieu to the man she was walking with and get into a taxi with another boy. She recollected how Arup and she would often take a rickshaw back home after seeing off friends. She looked around for the car in which Sahana was travelling. Her brother would have been so proud to see the fine woman his daughter had grown into.

As the car moved ahead, she saw buildings that had not changed much. There was a lot of order in everything that she saw, but the old warmth seemed missing. Dacca was bearing the burden of being a capital city, she thought. She crossed the large park where she would often go with her grandfather. The feel of his strong arms as he carried her around, and his thick fingers, which she held while walking, were still fresh in her mind. Her grandfather was widely respected in Dacca. She loved the adulation her grandfather received as the two walked in the park. She felt like a princess whenever she was with him. Her park had changed a lot. It had many swings and merry-go-rounds installed in place of the small play areas. It was more tranquil earlier, but then so was Dacca.

The driver stopped the car near the old market. The market, a few kilometers away from the hospital where she practiced as a doctor, had many shops that she used to visit. Her clinic, which she had set up in her final years in Dacca, was also there. Several new buildings had come up, but surprisingly, most of the old ones were still intact, some dilapidated, some still looked strong. Anxious to see the state of her clinic, she looked around and saw a pharmacy in its place. The board on top read, 'Paki Pharmacy.' She looked at Samina and started laughing.

'It was my daughter Salma's idea, not mine. She has started a small nursing home. We did not want to sell this place. It was her idea to convert it into a pharmacy and name it Paki Pharmacy,' Samina spoke, starting in a sheepish tone but ending with laughter.

Damyanti saw a small tailoring shop in one of the buildings. Remembering how often Samina and she went to that shop to get their dresses stitched, she walked towards it briskly. Like every other place, the shop had also become crowded. It had more people and sewing machines than she remembered.

'Is Masterji there?' she asked a small boy sitting near the shutter.

'Yes,' he replied and went inside.

A middle-aged man came out.

'May I help you?' he asked.

'Can you please call the Masterji?' she asked again.

'I'm the tailor master of this shop.'

'No, I mean the old man.'

Samina, amused with the conversation, tapped her shoulders gently, and said, 'Paki, everyone is not as unwelcome in Allah's abode as you and me. It has been 40 years and Masterji was a very old man at that time. This is his grandson. And the boy you spoke to is his great grandson.'

Damyanti stood still. 'Yes, it has been 40 years', she spoke to herself.

'Samin, can you lend me 500 *taka*?' she requested her friend.

She handed over the money to the young boy, caressed his head and told him, 'Buy some sweets and toys for yourself. Your great-grandfather was a very nice man.'

***

Salma had made arrangements for everyone's stay in her own house and across houses of various family members.

Salim, who died a bachelor, had left his house to Bashir's sons. The house, which remained locked most of the time, was cleaned and prepared for this occasion. Following the footsteps of his father and grandfather, Bashir's eldest son had joined the army.

Damyanti's house had changed a few hands. The last owners had demolished the old building and built a new house. Every time that the house was put up for sale, Samina had wanted to buy it. But the quoted price had always been beyond her reach. So, when the last owners were migrating to Canada three years back, she broached the topic with Razaq. Since he was settled in London, she did not expect him to show any willingness to buy it. But to her delight, he flew to Dacca and closed the deal by quoting ten per cent more than a deal which was almost closed. He was accused by property dealers of spoiling the real estate market on the strength of English pounds. No one understood the emotion behind this seemingly irrational decision, a son's desire to see happiness and a sense of satisfaction on his mother's face. The house was freshly painted in the same colours as that of Damyanti's original house.

Though the family members stayed in different houses, they assembled for breakfast, lunch, and dinner at Samina's.

Everyone had so much to catch up on. Discussions were full of questions, and each answer, however detailed, led to many more questions. Occasionally, some old wound would open up, only to heal quickly with the reassuring presence of family and loved ones. Older people relived memories, the younger ones watched with fascination. And the younger ones presented fresh views, so divergent from the traditional, as the elders heard with rapt attention. Almost everyone had a connection with Dacca, and those who did not, felt there had been some relationship waiting to be unraveled. New friendships were being forged. In Samina's daughter Salma, Sahana did not only find a fellow doctor but also a soul sister. Salma's son and Damyanti's grandson Soumen got along very well. Everyone loved Bashir's widow and was very appreciative of her untiring effort in ensuring that everyone was comfortable. Damyanti's daughter-in-law Sarika extended an invitation to Bashir's widow to visit Lucknow and stay with them.

On the second day of her stay, Damyanti expressed her desire to visit the graves of Salim, Samina's husband Iqbal, and her son Bashir, only to realize that she was prohibited as a woman to enter the graveyard. Samina and she decided to visit the memorial built in memory of Salim, a prominent political leader in his final years, and the War Memorial built in memory of the heroes who had died fighting for the liberation of Bangladesh. It was decided that they would pass by the graveyard and maybe spend a few minutes outside.

'Samin, Salim should have married,' she spoke softly as the two stood in front of his statue. Samina stayed silent and extended her hand to hold her friend's hand. Holding each other's hands tightly, the two walked back in silence.

They went to the National Martyr's Memorial after that. Damyanti had decided not to break down in front of Samina, but could not hold herself. The two hugged each other and cried. The memorial reminded her of Bashir, the child she had loved as her own. She remembered how he played in her lap for hours and often slept next to her before her own sons were born. 'No one deserves to die so young. How cruel has it been for my friend and Bashir's widow,' she thought. 'Those *outsiders*....'

They went to the graveyard where Salim was buried. The three women got out of the car.

Struggling to hold her emotion, Damyanti pleaded, 'Samin, I want to go inside. Please arrange for me to go at least once. I want to spend a few minutes next to Salim's body.'

'Paki, you know that we can't.'

'Please, Samin. Once. Please bribe the keeper but arrange for me to go in once.'

'Bribe? Is that you, Paki. Our honest and upright Paki,' Parineeta said with laughter.

Samina walked towards Damyanti, held her in her arms and the two began sobbing uncontrollably.

Damyanti came away with a regret that she could not visit the grave.

In the next few days, she went around the town. She

was surprised to see that although most were born after she had left Dacca, they had heard about her and had stories to share. Most of them knew her as Doctor Madam, a few as Communist *Didi*, and everyone as the granddaughter of Late Dinanath.

The three friends went to the ground they played in as kids. The area had shrunk, giving up space for construction of houses. Damyanti looked around as if she was searching for something. 'Paki, are you looking for the large drums we used to hide behind?' Samina spoke with a twinkle. 'Or, maybe she is looking for the pit where we would beat her in the game of marbles and she would run to Salim complaining.' Parineeta added with laughter. Lost in her thoughts, Damyanti exclaimed, 'Oh! The pillar is still there.' The broad pillar, which was at the center of the ground, then, now occupied most of the grounds. Also intact was the Banyan tree next to the pillar. The majestic tree and the pillar brought back sweet memories to Damyanti. The friends would sit below the banyan tree to cool off after play. As she looked at the pillar and tree, memories of discussions, fights, and arguments that the friends had had during childhood came to her mind. This was the place where she would hold court like a regal princess.

Damyanti walked silently towards the tree and pillar. She plucked six leaves from the Banyan tree and put it in her handbag. Then, she bent down, collected some dry mud and wrapped it in a piece of paper and put it beside the leaves. She took a rough edged stone, walked towards the pillar, and slowly etched on it, 'Pari, Samin, Paki. December 15, 1986. Missing Salim, Arup and Tapan this day.'

With moist eyes, she walked towards the car.

The friends visited their school. Almost everything had changed school uniform and even the way the students came across now. Damyanti was pleasantly surprised to see her name displayed proudly along with a few other select names on a board with a golden boundary. It read, 'Damyanti Ghosh, 1918-1929 – First doctor from the school. First rank all classes.'

When the school Principal came to know of Damyanti's visit to the school, she hurriedly called for school assembly in the middle of the day. In front of Damyanti, whose tears were refusing to stop, the students first sang the new school song and then a Rabindra Sangeet.

Never in her long life had Damyanti felt as proud as she did standing in front of those kids, speaking to them in the assembly.

She visited Gurudwara Nanak Shahi along with Paramjit and his wife. On their way back, they saw a small rest house for pilgrims, very close to the *gurudwara*. The building looked old and dilapidated. There was a stone firmly fixed at the entrance. The inscription on the stone mentioned the names of three donors. The first name, written in a larger font than the other two, was 'Davinder

Dussanj'. Paramjit rushed towards the house and wiped the stone with his handkerchief. He bowed in front of the stone, touched it with his forehead and started crying. The house did not have an owner and was managed by the *gurudwara*. He met the members of the *gurudwara* committee and offered to pay for the complete renovation of the building. To his surprise, the committee offered to name the building 'Davinder Nilay'. Damyanti had rarely seen him as happy as that day.

A day before Damyanti's departure, an event was organized by Karim-Dinanath Bangla Sahitya Sammelan. The audience was elated to find members of Late Dinanath's family amongst them. The event was attended by prominent poets, writers, and many distinguished people of Dacca. As the event was drawing to a close, overwhelmed with emotion, Razaq proposed that an annual award for female debut writers be instituted in the names of Damyanti and his mother. He offered to donate a sum of money every year. The proposal was met with loud cheer from everyone in the audience. And then, a few more people stood up to commit money towards the award, among them were Damyanti's elder son Soumitro and Samina's nephews. The crowd was surprised to see a young boy raise his hand. Holding the hands of his grandmother and Samina, Soumen, with tears in his eyes, promised to pay ten thousand *taka* every year from the day he would start working.

In the seven days that Damyanti spent in Dacca, she lived the forty years she had missed. The night before she left, the three friends remained awake, talking all night long. On the way to the airport, they cried away from the eyes of others. Damyanti knew she would never be able to see Dacca again and was extremely thankful to her niece Sahana for planning this visit. As she got down from the car, she hugged Samina and Parineeta, and then kneeled on the ground to kiss it. She kissed it for a long time, and when she got up, a part of her beautiful land was deeply soaked with her tears.

Chapter 13

The trip to Dacca was invigorating for Damyanti. It seemed to have reversed the process of aging for her. She looked healthier and younger. The boys were in colleges, leaving her time to introspect and analyze. As India was witnessing a change in political equations, she was looking at the days ahead with hope and anxiety.

In the new cabinet formed after the 1985 general election, Vishwanath Pratap Singh was appointed as finance minister by Rajiv Gandhi. As finance minister, V P Singh began framing policies that were hurting businessmen who had been donors to the Congress for decades. He raided many of them for evading taxes. The party needed funds on a continuous basis and could not afford the wrath and alienation of these businessmen. He had become an albatross around Rajiv Gandhi's neck. But sacking V P Singh could have created a furor amongst the public and hence Rajiv moved him as the Defense Minister.

The Defense ministry was dependent on foreign manufacturers for procuring arms and ammunitions. Large value deals were suspected to involve payments as kickbacks to politicians and army officers. V P Singh started investigating deals concluded in the past and was rumored to have found certain documents related to the procurement of the Bofors 155 mm Field Howitzer. Afraid that the investigation could incriminate Rajiv Gandhi, Singh was sacked from the ministry in three months. Singh resigned from the Congress and the Lok Sabha, and with time became the rallying force against the prime minister.

Damyanti was watching these developments with interest and anxiety.

On completion of her schooling, Riyaz's sister Saira, the youngest of Damyanti's group of kids and the most pampered by her, took admission in Standard XI in Delhi Public School, New Delhi. Influenced by a cousin who had studied there and was a budding journalist, she had been persistent on studying in DPS. Belying everyone's expectation, she aggregated a 91.7% and won the ticket to the school of her dreams.

During the winter vacation in December, Soumen, Bhola, Ravi, and Saira travelled together to Patna. The friends had a great time during the journey, playing games and eating snacks. Soumen left no stones unturned to ensure that Saira was comfortable. While everyone went to sleep in the night, the two barely slept, chatting all along.

The environment in India had begun to change. The

demand for the site for the Ram temple was becoming more strident. Political parties were becoming regional, each trying to consolidate its identified voter base.

Little did Damyanti's boys know then that these changes would impact them directly, creating turmoil and pain in their lives.

V P Singh came to power in 1989, riding on the Bofors wave.

By December 1989, Soumen was in his final year at IIT, Delhi, and applying to universities in the US for admission in a post-graduate programme. Ravi and Bhola had completed graduation and were admitted to Delhi University for post-graduation. Both had written the civil services exam. While Ravi had cleared the preliminary exams and was awaiting results for the mains, Bhola had failed to clear the first. Clearing the Indian Civil Services examination was becoming tougher each year, adding to their fear. Determined to make to the final list, seats for which were very few, Ravi had shut doors to any other options. Saira had completed her Grade 12, and again, belying everyone's expectation, obtained very high marks. She had secured an admission in Lady Shriram College. Madhav was enjoying his time in IIT, Kanpur, deeply immersed in studies with the constant guidance and support from Soumen.

Unlike earlier, the friends could not travel together to Patna during winter vacations that year. Soumen and Saira stayed back, telling everyone they needed to finish some important assignments and then took a train together a week later. During the entire train journey, the two kept chatting. Dressed in a pair of blue jeans, a t-shirt, and a woolen sweater, Saira had wrapped herself with a maroon shawl gifted to her by Soumen.

The old woman sleeping from across them would occasionally look at the two from the corner of her eyes, smiled and blessed them.

Saira had grown into a beautiful woman, full of warmth and compassion. Very fair, tall at 5 ft 6 in, with shoulder length, thick black hair, slender body and intense eyes — she could easily be mistaken for a model. Intelligent and well read, she could talk on diverse topics. A student of political science, she wanted to work in the area of public policy.

Damyanti and Rehana, Saira's mother, were at the Patna station to receive them. The two got down from the train and touched Damyanti's feet to seek her blessings. Then, Soumen greeted Rehana with folded hands as Saira rushed to hug her. After the initial greetings, the four walked towards the exit. Seeing Soumen and Saira walk beside each other, Damyanti smiled, recalling herself and Gautam all those years ago.

In the one month that Saira spent in Patna, she came to meet Damyanti almost every day. She spent a lot of time with her, either chatting or learning to cook Bengali dishes. And whether they spoke in the kitchen or living room, Soumen was always there. At the time of leaving, she would make it a point to spend fifteen minutes with Soumen in his room. The two always ensured that the door to his room was wide open.

It did not take Damyanti long to understand that the two were in love. Strangely, they reminded her of so much that she had locked in her heart. Looking at them, she saw a long and tough battle ahead.

She wanted to broach the topic with Soumen and was waiting for an opportune moment. Not having found the right one and anxious that he would leave for Delhi, she couldn't help but ask him two days before his departure. 'Do you like Saira, Soumen?'

Alarmed at the question, he replied without raising his eyes from the book he was reading, 'Yes, she is very intelligent. An admission in LSR is no mean achievement.'

'I mean, are you looking at building a future with her?'

There was a long silence and then, he just said, '*Thakurma.*'

Damyanti did not pursue the discussion further. It ended as abruptly as it had begun. Both knew that the brief sentences had met their purpose and was the beginning of long discussions that they would eventually engage in, in due course.

By the summer of 1990, Soumen had secured an admission in Stanford University for an MS. He was supposed to join the varsity in the middle of September and had planned to leave for the US towards the end of August. Ravi had failed to clear the civil services and was contemplating writing it again that year. Bhola had decided not to attempt the examination that year and instead write for the Bihar Public Services Commission. Riyaz was close to becoming a doctor and was excited to serve in the army.

Them, Soumen's friends at IIT, and Saira's at LSR knew this was no ordinary infatuation of a boy and a girl who had grown up together. It was deep love. There was no one who did not believe that the two were meant to be together.

***

Ravi became depressed when he couldn't clear the civil services and was shocked to know that Mahendra, four years senior to him, and a topper, had also failed to make it.

Janata Dal's victory in the state elections in Bihar and Uttar Pradesh, after a spectacular show in the Lok Sabha elections in north India, strengthened V P Singh's belief that his vote base lay in the Hindi heartland. He was worried that the VHP's campaign for the Ram *Mandir*, supported by the BJP, had grown very strong. The movement was consolidating Hindus in favor of the BJP and Singh understood that if this translated to votes for the Hindu nationalist party, it could finish his political career. A division of Hindu votes would weaken the BJP.

Ravi had barely come out of depression when on August 7, 1990, V P Singh announced in Parliament that his government had decided to implement the Mandal Commission Report. The report recommended a 27% reservation for Other Backward Castes (OBC) in government services. Members of the OBC were a large vote bank, and this was viewed as a masterstroke.

Ravi had planned a small dinner that day to celebrate his birthday.

When Bhola walked in with Ram Charan, a member of the Schedule Caste community, the environment in the room had no semblance of a party. There were bottles of whisky and Old Monk in the corner. The glasses were full and so were the bottles. Although the boys had poured their drinks, it seemed that none had touched his glass. The discussions ended abruptly the moment the two walked in. Bhola hugged Ravi with a lot of warmth, but to his surprise the latter remained stiff.

The discussion in the room and the overall gloom thereafter was a mirror image of what was happening in Delhi University and other parts of India.

Mahendra was the last person to walk in. Barely able to speak in his inebriated condition, he slurred, 'Ravi, what's the name of your friend who got into IAS on SC/ST reserved category?'

'Mohan, Mahen *Bhaiya*. I have rarely seen you drunk. Hope all is well?' Ravi replied, catching Mahendra by his forearm lest he fell down.

'Yes, Mohan. I am sure I will have to work as a BDO reporting to him. Ravi, can you please request him to be lenient towards me when he becomes my boss?' he spoke with biting sarcasm.

'*Bhaiya*, this time you will get through IAS. Don't worry.'

Mahendra threw the book he was holding. It hit the wall and came down with a thud.

'No, Ravi. Our dear Prime Minister has ensured that our dreams remain dreams. We worked so hard for his election campaign after his men came to us, seeking help in the name of JP *babu*, and claimed that he was different from other politicians. He showed so much promise as finance minister and vowed to do so much for us. But once the colour is off, the fox is revealed. He is just like any other politician, maybe worse than most,' Mahendra spoke with more pain than anger.

A few more friends joined the discussion. Everyone spoke with anger and hurt. The speeches were acerbic and it became awkward for Bhola and Ram Charan to remain in the room.

Mahendra, who was struggling to remain seated because of the amount of alcohol he had consumed, lost balance, fell on the ground, and puked. The disruption caused took everyone out of the heated discussion. The boys had planned to go to a nearby *dhaba* for dinner after having their drinks, but no one had any appetite left. Bhola was quiet right through; as a probable beneficiary of the Mandal Commission Report, maybe he was reluctant to react.

The party ended with the boys leaving.

Ravi and his roommate were left alone.

'My chances of getting into the IAS is almost nil now,' Ravi was incoherent, tears in his eyes.

A couple of weeks later, a large group of students took out a procession against the proposed implementation of the Mandal Commission Report. There were hundreds of students out on the streets. Amongst them was Ravi, inconspicuous, disillusioned, dejected, and disturbed. In the following weeks, the processions became more frequent. In many cases, students resorted to violence, causing damage and destruction. The hope that the government might rescind was quickly turning to despair. And as the aggression of students increased, the inconspicuous Ravi became one of the most prominent activists. Unlike some, his involvement was only due to his frustration, which kept increasing with the apathy of the government.

***

Soumen had booked his tickets to fly from Delhi to Stanford. Aware of the unrest in Delhi, Damyanti wanted him to fly from Bombay. But he had promised Saira he would meet her before flying to the US and a ticket from Bombay would have made that impossible. It was finally agreed that Damyanti would accompany him to Delhi and return the next day.

Soumen and Damyanti reached Delhi the evening before the day of his departure and checked into a hotel close to the airport. Saira joined them for breakfast the next morning. The moment she entered the hotel room, Damyanti took her in her arms, hugged her, and kissed her forehead. She was dressed in a white *churidar*, deep green *kameez*, and a white *dupatta*. Damyanti kept looking at her, admiring her beauty, elegance and confidence. The three spent the entire day together, most of the time shopping for things Soumen would need in Stanford. Saira had a final say in everything. She decided on the number of woolen clothes that he needed to carry, even the colours that she thought would look good on him. She persuaded him to buy a black blazer apart from the navy blue that he already had. Expecting some last minute shopping, she had carried with her two Samsonite bags. None of these went unnoticed by Damyanti.

The flight was scheduled to depart late in the night. In the evening, Damyanti excused herself so that the young lovers could spend some time alone.

Soumen and Saira returned at 7:30 pm.

'*Thakurma*, Saira has come to say bye to you. She is going back to her hostel,' he told Damyanti as soon as they entered the room.

'Oh! Don't you want to see him off at the airport, *beta*?' Damyanti asked.

'But the flight is at 3 am, *dadi ma*. It may not be safe for me to travel at that time,' Saira answered, looking at Soumen.

'Why don't you stay with me tonight, *beta*? My flight is in the evening and you could leave after lunch. Anyway, tomorrow is Sunday. We will get to spend some time together after Soumen leaves.'

Saira nodded. Damyanti was struggling to hide her smile, and Saira and Soumen their excitement.

She handed over some money to Soumen and asked him to go with Saira and help her buy some nightwear.

Soumen's departure left a void in the hearts of Damyanti and Saira, as if a part of them had gone along with him. Tired and sad, Saira slept immediately after her return from the airport. Seated on the sofa beside the bed, Damyanti was watching her lovingly.

Saira was curled like a baby, her face towards Damyanti. She was wearing the pink nightwear. The girl, who looked like a confident woman a few hours ago appeared so vulnerable now. The blanket was carelessly covering half her body, and as she turned, it slipped off completely. The air from AC vent was directed towards the bed, and as she lay exposed to it, she curled further.

Damyanti got up from her seat, switched off the table lamp, put the blanket softly on Saira's body, and sat next to her. Saira opened her eyes for a moment, smiled, and went off to sleep. Caressing her hair gently, Damyanti asked her, not expecting a reply, '*Beta*, do you love Soumen?'

'Yes, *dadi*.'

'Do you want to marry him?'

Saira opened her eyes, half in sleep, and replied, 'Yes, *dadi*.' She snuggled close to Damyanti and went into deep sleep.

Damyanti bent and kissed her forehead. And at that moment, she made a promise to herself that she would ensure that Soumen and Saira married each other.

***

Ravi had been confident that the government would retract its position on the implementation of Mandal Commission Report. But the government remained passive, and by the middle of September, Ravi had begun to lose hope. He became more and more reticent, cutting himself off socially and limiting himself to a few friends, who were as dejected as he was.

Ravi, Madhav, and Bhola came to Patna during *Durga Puja*. Unlike earlier, the three travelled on different days. Damyanti was surprised to see Madhav alighting alone from the train and was astonished to learn that the three friends had not even bothered to check about each other's plans. The aloofness, cold vibes, and discomfort between them troubled her; she felt defeated, as if someone, some unknown evil force had given her a body blow, a strong, hard, painful one.

She called Ravi and Bhola for lunch on *Vijayadashmi*. Seated a little away from each other, the boys were struggling to find topics for discussion. She once again observed their discomfort with each other and called Madhav to the other room to find out what was wrong.

'I'm not sure, *dadi*. I know Ravi is very disturbed and sees the Mandal Commission Report as an end to his ambition. Ravi and Bhola have had bitter arguments on this.

Ravi has hardly spoken since he has come and seems to be in a constant state of depression.'

Madhav's reply made Damyanti more anxious. She asked Ravi to stay after Bhola left. On her prodding, Ravi told her about his fears. He seemed to have lost all hope, inflicting immense pain upon himself. She was worried for him and concerned that his depression might drive him to doing something insane.

'Ravi, we often mistake a battle for a war. Life is a long journey and losing a battle is no indication of how life may eventually turn into. At times, we give up very easily, burdened and troubled by an incident or a series of events in quick succession. But we don't realize that there could be something better in the future. I'll tell you my own experience and would urge you to be strong, not to yield to one-time setbacks, however big they may seem to be.'

He was listening to her intently.

'I had never thought of a life outside Dacca. I had always wanted to be close to my relatives and friends. My neighborhood was one of the finest examples of communal harmony. My family was one of the most reputed in the whole of East Bengal. And then, one day, my entire world was turned upside down...' she continued, looking out into the distance.

She took a long pause, looked at the floor below, and spoke softly, 'I've not told anyone what I'm telling you now. On the way to the relief camp, twice I thought of ending my life. I had almost made up my mind to drown myself the first time and consume poison the second. I thought there was nothing left in life. All was lost. I was in a state of constant depression.'

Ravi had tears in his eyes as he listened to her. She continued speaking, regaining the strength in her voice.

'And then, one day, I came across a woman much younger than me in the camp. She had lost her husband and one-year-old son. She did not know anyone and had no one to go to. But to my utter surprise, she was busy helping everyone. In those few days, she had become an anchor to the orphaned children. When I looked at her, my own sorrow looked so small. I decided at that moment that I would not give up. Today, when I look back, I feel sad that I had to leave Dacca. But, I have so many reasons to be happy about, so many things that I have received from this new place I made my home all those years ago. I have been able to help many people and have received lots of love. And importantly, I got a chance to be with my wonderful boys, all of you.'

She came closer to him, squeezed his hand, and said, 'Ravi, never give up. Something beautiful may be there in future and we need to give that a chance by being patient and by fighting back. *Beta*, things will be fine. Do not give up...'

Ravi felt better and relaxed, but only till he reached Delhi. He was back amongst his friends and the same discussions. The protests intensified with students, demanding an assurance on the rollback from none less than V P Singh. But Singh remained firm.

The results of the preliminary examination of civil services were published in October. Many students feared it could be the last examination before the implementation of the Mandal Commission Report. Ravi was devastated to find his roll number missing from the list. He went back into a shell. He became a constant participant in all the protest marches and most of the time was in the front.

On October 20, a large number of students took a protest march to the precincts of South Block and began shouting for the rollback of the Report. The area was cordoned off by the police force. The students made an attempt to reach the Secretariat building, but were pushed back. Someone shouted for the Prime Minister to come out and meet them. Soon, that demand became a slogan. Amidst feverish sloganeering, someone shouted that he would burn himself if no one listened. And then, everyone started chanting that he would burn himself. Ravi was in the front, shouting and chanting. A couple of boys ran, took off the pipes from the fuel tanks of motorbikes, filled a few cans and rushed back. The protestors started shouting with the cans in hand, threatening to burn themselves if their demands were not met. The police moved ahead, attempting to take the cans away. Before anyone could react, amid high decibel slogans all around, Ravi snatched two cans from the protestors, emptied the petrol on his body, took out his cigarette lighter and the next moment was engulfed in flames. The students moved away from him in panic. By the time they realized what had happened and came to his rescue, Ravi's body was badly burnt. He was rushed to a nearby hospital and then shifted to AIIMS.

By the evening, Ravi had succumbed to his injuries.

***

Damyanti had acute pain in her chest that night and was rushed to PMCH. She was shattered by Ravi's death. She knew he was depressed, but had never imagined that he would take such a drastic step. She blamed herself for not having anticipated this, especially since she had met him less than a month back.

The feeling of failure was sinking her. As a child, she had only envisioned happy days. She was one of the few women doctors of her time, a very strong woman, and member of one of the most prominent families in Bengal. But wherever it mattered the most, where she should have reacted with all her strength, she felt she had always failed. This feeling of repeated failure was a burden that was only becoming heavier with each memory.

She could have joined politics — she was acknowledged as a strong leader — and fought men like Salman or maybe Jinnah, fought against the idea of division of Bengal and India. But she abandoned midway the fight that she had begun in college. A life in Dacca was what all her friends had wished for, but while Tapan, Arup, and Salim had made sacrifices for noble causes, she had chosen domesticity in Dacca.

She could have gone back to Dacca and lived there, like so many Hindus did post-independence of Bangladesh. Undoubtedly, the massacre in Noakhali was extremely painful, heart wrenching, but didn't she accept defeat too early by moving to Patna, by not giving the common people another chance to prove that for them it simply did not matter that she was a Hindu and not a Muslim.

She cut off ties with Salim without explaining anything to him. She cut off all ties with her sister, Samina, after leaving Dacca. Was she not punishing Samina for the actions of a few criminals? Couldn't she have explained things to Salim, if not then, then maybe later?

She saw Gautam die in excruciating pain. He lived a difficult and torturous life in jail, while she had lived a life of comfort in her home. She had seen him cough badly six months before his release, but had missed to read that it could have been tuberculosis.

Babban was dead, murdered. She had been helpless.

She had wished for a life of friendship for her boys. She had been more than a parent to them, teaching them the right values and tried to make them sensitive and strong. But both Daljit and Ravi failed. In both cases, she had had an opportunity to prevent the deaths, but had failed.

She had toiled hard to strengthen the friendship that the boys had, but her last meeting with Bhola, Ravi, and Madhav had been disappointing. The boys were awkward, as if they did not want to be in the same room. Was her teaching so weak that it could not withstand a small storm?

Politicians had succeeded in creating fissures in the society and, sadly, amongst her boys.

Damyanti felt overwhelmed, her confidence crushed. Was she actually helpless or had she allowed the situations to overwhelm her? Couldn't she have stood against the forces in her own small way? Did she fail in reading situations in front of her? Did she fail to take stands? As scary thoughts kept attacking her, the pain in her chest moved to her head.

Her thoughts moved to Saira and Soumen. Was that going to be her next defeat? And would that defeat sink her further in her own eyes?

In that pain, she resolved she would never let such forces defeat her in the future; that she would fight back, however big and widespread the forces were. The missteps of the past would not be repeated in future. She could not afford another defeat.

She took a deep breath and sat down to write a letter to Samina.

'...*Samin, I've lost Arup and Tapan, once again. I have lost them again to divisive, greedy, and power-hungry people. Nothing seems to have changed in the last fifty years. In fact, things are worse. Thakurda used to say that there was a small section of outsiders wanting to disturb the harmony of Dacca. I fear we have outsiders everywhere, and they do not necessarily come from outside. I am scared that every corner might become a Dacca; a few wily men may divide innocent, gullible people and the fire may engulf everyone, sparing not even my children.*

I feel lost and defeated, tired and exhausted. Fate seems to be taking away everything from me again, the way it had half a century back. I had begun reliving my unfinished past through my kids, but alas! Oh! Maa Durga!

Sorry for this unpleasant letter, Samin. But whom else could I have poured my heart to? Who will understand what I'm going through, my sense of loss and despair?'

As she walked towards the postbox to drop the letter, Damyanti was bitter, sad, angry, but more determined than ever to fight back.

At that old age, she was readying herself for one last battle, one that she was determined to win; the one win that would help her redeem herself, at least to some extent, in her own eyes.

Chapter 14

The divisive rhetoric during the Mandal agitation and Ram Mandir movement further fractured an already divided society. These movements also saw the entry of religious and caste-based leaders into politics. Zafar, Saira's father, was often approached by leaders from his community for electoral endorsements and to participate in community specific events. He declined such requests, often with subtle resentment. He had distaste for people who used religion as a calling card, a lever.

But Zafar's strong beliefs were shaken the day BJP leader Lal Krishna Advani was arrested during the *rath yatra*. The news of the arrest made a section of people angry, creating widespread chaos. The resultant backlash was on innocent Muslims. Zafar was on his way home that evening, a few kilometers from his house, when two men barged to his car menacingly. Sensing danger, his driver increased the speed of the vehicle, but was limited by traffic and the narrowness of the road. The men started chasing the car. As the car slowed down at the bend near the petrol pump, the men drew close, took out sharp-edged knives neatly tucked in their trouser belts, and one of them hit the window. The glass cracked. The other man bent down, picked up a couple of large-sized stones and hit the window. The glass shattered into pieces. Zafar was watching with horror as the two men came closer with knives in their hands. Thankfully, the road after the bend was clear and the driver pressed the accelerator to the maximum. The car moved away at high speed, taking the attackers by surprise.

As the car sped, Zafar kept looking at the rear window. The men had started running behind the car. They were hurling abuses at him, with deep hatred in their eyes. The unexplained disgust that he saw in them and the hostility that drove them was something he was not able to comprehend. He kept praying as his driver struggled to negotiate sharp bends and avoid accidents. The distance between the two attackers, running like men possessed, and the car kept increasing. But uncertain of traffic conditions ahead, Zafar knew any moment could be his last.

When the men realized that catching up was impossible, they bent down, picked a couple of boulders and threw them at the car. Zafar looked at the swing of their arms with horror. By God's grace the boulders first fell on the boot and then hit the rear glass. The glass cracked as the boulders fell back with a thud.

Zafar got down from his car, shaken. Never had he

spoken a single sentence that could drive someone to such hatred and insanity. He was sure that the people who attacked him were aware of his identity. And that was what worried him most. He was attacked because he was Muslim; the two men never bothered to check what he stood for as Zafar. Those ten to fifteen minutes, locked in the car, praying for his life, uprooted his faith in several principles that he believed in. The near-death experience shook the very foundation of the ideals that he had held dear. The ugly behavior of the two men left several questions in his mind. He was aware that the two were not representative of the majority, but feared that they could be part of a swelling tribe.

The news of the attack spread like wildfire in his neighborhood and amongst the Muslim community. There was a stream of visitors the next day. Everyone that he knew from his neighborhood, university, and social circle was present. While people expressed their sympathy and support, the question that constantly plagued him was what if it happened again. Not confident of timely support from the police, he was worried if anyone would risk his own safety to intervene. When he was attacked, people had just stood by watching. Though hundreds came to express their solidarity, he felt isolated and victimized.

Also present among the visitors were Maulana Azhar, a religious leader, and Mir Ali, a local politician. Zafar had never met them apart from a couple of brief meetings at social occasions. Any other day he wouldn't have spent more than fifteen minutes with them, but that evening the two stayed back for dinner and left late in the night. What he would term as cloyingly sweet at any other time appeared genuine talk to him that day. Both Maulana and Mir spoke of things that he had always abhorred, but he found himself listening to them. They explained to him how only community members would step forward to help him and his family and how everyone in the community needed to unite against the Hindu forces. Rehana listened to them as well, but with little conviction. She was as shocked as Zafar with the ordeal that he had gone through and hence refrained from expressing her views.

Zafar's proximity to Maulana and Mir had not gone unnoticed by Damyanti, and she feared that he might allow himself to be manipulated by the two wily, self-serving men.

Disheartened with the environment around her and depressing headlines glaring out of the front pages of newspapers on the Ram Mandir movement, Damyanti was losing hope in the ability and intent of political leaders, and also in the courage of the general people.

Soumen travelled to India on a break in July. He stayed in Delhi for a few days and then, along with Saira, took a train to Patna. Saira had stayed back in Delhi during the summer vacation. She was working with an NGO on a project on public policy.

Unaware that Soumen was accompanying Saira, Zafar and Rehana were surprised to find Damyanti at Patna station. They were astonished to learn that Soumen was coming by the same train. They watched the young couple intently as the two got down together, Saira holding Soumen's hand with one hand for support and her bag in the other. The comfort between the two was unmistakable.

Rehana and Zafar had known Soumen from his childhood. They loved him. He was their son's closest friend and an embodiment of good behavior, intelligence, and humility. It had never occurred to them that their daughter might want to marry him. The thought of Saira marrying someone of 'another faith' worried them, afraid how society would react. The relationship between the two was an obvious topic of discussion between them and not hidden from the prying ears of maids and servants at home.

Soumen left for Calcutta after two weeks and then to Singapore for an internship.

Rehana and Zafar expected their discussion with Saira to be prolonged, but to their surprise it finished quickly. They spoke to her at length, stressing that children needed to be transparent with their parents and asked her if she liked Soumen. They expected her to deny it and had planned to insist that she be truthful.

But Saira replied, 'Yes, we want to marry each other.'

'But what about his being a Hindu?' Rehana uttered, immediately.

'What about it?' Saira asked, with the same simplicity.

'What will people say?'

'Which people?'

'Society. Neighbors. People we know…'

'I don't think I care beyond you and Riyaz.'

'Even we are not comfortable with the idea of you marrying a non-Muslim?'

'Not even Soumen? I've grown up hearing praises for him from the both of you.'

There was silence for some time and then Saira continued.

'*Ammi, Abba*, I love him. I know I will be happy with him. He respects me as much as he loves me. I am yet to meet someone who is such a gentleman. We are comfortable with each other. His thinking matches mine and he will help me flourish in whatever I choose to do.' She paused, looked at them, and said, 'If you differ on any of these points, let me know. Don't tell me not to marry him because he is not a Muslim.'

There was absolute silence. The discussion ended, leaving Rehana and Zafar stunned and confused.

Saira left for Delhi after a few days.

Gradually, from one house to another, the news spread in the neighborhood. And in due course, it reached Maulana and Mir. What was nothing more than pure love between two educated youngsters was coloured as communal and became a topic of discussion for community leaders and elders. Many came up to express their sympathies to Rehana and Zafar and some were extreme in their suggestions on how the situation should be dealt with. Strangely, the couple was mute listeners on such occasions, often lost for words.

Damyanti received a call from Rehana on August 14, asking if Zafar and she could meet her the next evening. Rehana's tone was apprehensive, uneasy, and awkward. Expecting them to talk about Saira and Soumen, Damyanti prayed for the young couple several times that day. With folded hands in front of the portrait of Ma Durga, she pleaded for Rehana and Zafar's approval.

Ramu was asked to cook *mutton biryani* for the guests and get *sandesh* from the old Bengali sweet shop near the railway station.

Damyanti was surprised to see that Rehana and Zafar were accompanied by two men who she failed to recognize. After a brief exchange of pleasantries and discussion on political environment, Zafar brought up the topic that he had been waiting for.

'*Chachi*, we would like to discuss Saira and Soumen.'

Though she was expecting this, Damyanti was caught unawares by the suddenness of the statement. She shifted her gaze to Zafar and nodded.

'I'm not sure if you are aware that Saira and Soumen want to marry.'

She was waiting for him to continue, only to realize that the pause was actually a stop. He looked at her, expecting a reaction.

'Yes, I'm aware, but not completely. I'll be very happy to see them together,' she replied with a straight face, unsure how her enthusiasm would get viewed.

'But *chachi*, they are of different religions,' Rehana muttered.

'So?'

'It will be so difficult. They are from different backgrounds. They will never be compatible.'

Damyanti thought for some time and spoke, 'Rehana, I know the kids as much as you do, maybe more. You speak about different backgrounds, but take a closer look — the way they have been brought up, their education, ambition, friends — and you will observe that they have similar backgrounds. They have more similarities than differences.' She stared out of the window for some time and continued, 'In fact, the only difference that I see, among so many similarities, is religion.'

Maulana, visibly restless, interrupted, 'We can't have our girl marrying a Hindu boy. Never.'

Mir added, 'Not even if he adopts Islam.'

Damyanti was shocked. It took her sometime to gain back her composure. She looked at Zafar and said, 'Zafar, I've met almost all your relatives. I'm sorry, I fail to recognize these two men.'

'Sorry *chachi*, I forgot to introduce them. This is Maulana Azhar and this is Mir Ali. They are leaders of our community.'

'Our community!' she muttered softly.

She turned to the two men, 'Maulana and Mir *saab*, I'm very happy to meet leaders like you. The community needs a lot to be done around education, women empowerment, etc., and I am sure leaders like you two are busy with that. This specific issue is between two individuals and only between them. We don't have a role in this, neither you, nor me.'

'No, this cannot happen. It is not as per religion. Our daughter will suffer, our community will suffer. It is not in her interest,' Maulana, incoherent, was speaking with raised voice.

'Maulana *saab*, I'm not aware of your background, educational, or professional. We are talking about two youngsters who have had the privilege of going to the finest institutes in the country. They are informed, intelligent, and smart, and have had the opportunity to interact with some of the finest brains. I am sure their experience makes them more informed and aware than us. And, I've no doubt that they know what is right for them,' Damyanti was terse.

Maulana tried interrupting. Damyanti raised her hand, waved at them, and said, 'I have no role in this. Sorry, I can't discuss this any further.'

Maulana stood up in a jolt. 'Okay, we will leave then.'

'Ramu has cooked *mutton biryani*. I request you to have some. His *mutton biryani* is very tasty. You may ask Zafar.'

Zafar was still sitting, stunned. Maulana held his arm, pulled him, and said, 'Let's go.'

The four began walking towards the main door.

'Maulana *saab*,' Damyanti spoke in a slow but firm tone. 'You said, *our daughter*. I have spent thousands of hours with Saira. Zafar and Rehana know she is the apple of my eyes. She is my child, not yours. You don't know her. Don't demean her intelligence and my relationship with her.'

She shouted for Ramu and asked him to shut the door.

The meeting ended abruptly, leaving her with a splitting headache. She walked to the portrait of Ma Durga and touched her feet. With tears in her eyes, she pleaded, 'Ma, please give me strength. I cannot lose this battle. I have lost many. But not this one...'

***

Damyanti was worried, with scary and ugly thoughts cramming her mind. Soumen was away in a foreign land, too far off to fight this battle. Also, Saira and he were innocent youngsters, not adept in dealing with wily men like Maulana and Mir. She knew this battle had to be fought by her and only her.

Would she be able to fight this to the last or abandon it without a fight like in the case of Salim; or leave it midway, tired or drawn by other priorities, like the forum against the division of Bengal, like her battle to get Gautam released from prison?

Would Soumen meet the same fate as Ravi by taking away his life, frustrated, left with no hope? Would she make mistakes in reading the situation like she had in the case of Daljit and fail to act at the right time? Would people on the other side make her feel helpless, weak and inept like in Noakhali, in Punjab, during Emergency, and so many other occasions, big and small?

Frightened by such thoughts, with folded hands, eyes closed, she made a promise to Ma Durga that she would fight to the last and win.

***

The news of the visit spread faster than Damyanti had anticipated. After five days, two young men with saffron-colored cloth wrapped around their necks came to meet her. They introduced themselves as members of Hindu Suraksha Bal. The right-wing group had heard about the visit and feared that a lack of action from them might be viewed negatively by their followers. The environment was tense because of the agitation for the Ram Mandir. As leaders of one community looked at the other with suspicion and hatred, there were talks about a small section of members wanting to demolish the Babri Masjid.

Not completely aware of the discussions between the two families, they wanted Damyanti to say no to her grandson marrying a Muslim. And if Maulana and Mir had vehemently opposed the union, they wanted to extend their full support in getting them married, as per Hindu customs. The leaders of the Bal were worried that if Maulana and Mir succeeded, it could adversely affect the morale of their members, a disaster at the crucial juncture of the Ram Mandir movement.

Damyanti heard them patiently and quickly understood the perilous consequence of engaging in a conversation. She did not want to give them room for manipulation, cognizant that this was one battle best fought by keeping away from the battlefield.

'Thank you so much. Don't worry, I may look weak, but can fight many Maulanas and Mirs, if challenged,' Damyanti laughed loudly. 'My grandson is an intelligent boy and so is the girl. They are mature enough to understand what is right for them. No one has any right to interfere in something that is so personal between the two. And mind you, that includes Maulana, Mir, you, and even me.' She abruptly got up. 'You should taste the *payas* I cooked yesterday. Soumen and Saira love it.' She walked into the kitchen briskly and got two large bowls. As the boys ate, she switched the conversation to their education and career. She scolded them for not putting the right focus on their career and advised them on what they should be doing.

The two boys left completely outmaneuvered. If only she was more prepared for Zafar and Rehana's visit, the outcome could have been different. She had never expected the meeting to go the way it had, flummoxed by the inclusion of Maulana and Mir in the discussion. That Rehana and Zafar were apprehensive about the relationship did not come as a surprise to her, but that they were so deeply opposed did.

She vowed that she would not be outsmarted again. She was determined to play the game for Soumen and Saira. And play it smarter than the likes of Maulana, Mir, and members of the Bal.

A fortnight later, she went to Zafar's house unannounced, lest Maulana and Mir joined in. Ramu accompanied her, carrying two large boxes of *sandesh* and a big bowl of *payas*.

Zafar and Rehana appeared weak in their arguments and most of the times were parroting what the Maulana and Mir had said. Their words lacked conviction. They did not seem angry or upset, but tense, afraid, and helpless. Any other time, they would have been happy to see her.

'*Chachi*, I can't let my daughter marry outside of our community.'

'Who is your community, Zafar?'

Zafar was silent, so was Rehana.

'We are a part of the same community, Zafar. Look at yourself. Look at your neighbors and me. Look at the college you teach at or the school where Rehana teaches. Think of the people you interact with daily. And now look at the Maulana and Mir. Please ask yourself whom you identify with more? Please give me an honest answer.'

Zafar and Rehana kept looking at the ground.

'Rehana, a couple of weeks back two men from the Hindu Suraksha Bal came to my house. It did not take me long to realize that they are not a part of the same community as me. You and I belong to one community. How can religion, which is personal and private, a matter of faith, be the only factor to determine the community I belong to?'

'*Chachi*, I was chased by two men wielding knives. I could have been killed. If you had been chased similarly, I'm sure your views wouldn't have been very different from mine.'

Damyanti spoke with deep sadness. 'Zafar, the men who chased you, the men who came to meet me from the Bal, Maulana and Mir belong to one community. Please understand, you and I are not a part of that.'

She took a deep breath and continued, 'You lost hope after one ugly experience, leaving you with so much bitterness. Long back, stuck in a small room in Noakhali, I saw death and mayhem for a full week. My relatives got raped and butchered by Muslim men. Many were forced to convert to Islam. To this date, I have never hated anyone more. I still carry that hatred and it extends to people like them, irrespective of religion. But the barbarity of those few could never lessen my affection for the hundreds of Muslim men and women that I have known. To me, they belong to two different tribes. Over the years, I have learnt that religion is not a matter of identity, but only of personal faith. It is supposed to bind you to your god and not to other men.'

Damyanti continued for a long time. Conscious that her views and arguments were not cutting much ice with the couple, she moved the discussion to Soumen.

'Don't you like Soumen?'

'Of course, we do,' Rehana replied immediately. 'I have always given his example to Riyaz as an embodiment of right values.'

'Do you think he won't keep Saira happy? Will he not be a good husband to her?'

Rehana and Zafar were silent again. Damyanti paused for some time and spoke again, 'Do you think she will ever be happy if you get her married to someone else? You will not only be unfair to Saira and Soumen but also to the man she may marry.'

She got up from the sofa and walked towards the door. The couple struggled to lift themselves, weighed down by conflicting emotions.

She could understand that Zafar and Rehana saw reason in her words, but seemed helpless. And when they said that they needed to speak to people, she understood they would speak only to Maulana and Mir. It was evident that they would never say yes to the relationship, but seemed sure that their daughter would lead a happy life with Soumen.

She had not failed completely in her objective.

She came back home to the portrait of Ma Durga.

'Maa, I feel defeated, full of despair. How can I let men who attacked my family in Noakhali; men who created the divide between the people of two communities in Dacca, people who had only known how to live in peace; men who divided Bengal in 1905 and again in 1947 along with the Partition of India; men who tortured and killed my Bashir and my brothers and sisters in Bangladesh; men who snatched away Tapan and Arup; wily men who pushed Daljit, Ravi, and Babban to death defeat me once again? Those men, and Maulana, Mir, the current greedy politicians and men of the Bal are the same people. Ma, I cannot die with shaken faith, a feeling of defeat and low self-esteem. Please help me defeat these forces once, help me redeem myself in my own eyes.'

What Damyanti did not tell Ma, but was deep-seated in her heart, was that through the marriage of Saira and Soumen she also wished to correct a wrong that she had inflicted upon Salim and herself seventy years ago. What she had failed to do as child, overwhelmed by what she had seen, the burden of which she carried forever and which had magnified with the knowledge that Salim had remained unmarried, she could not let repeat. Saira and Soumen's marriage would give her a feeling of partial vindication. And, maybe make Salim's soul forgive her.

She took a train to Lucknow to meet Sarika and Sumanta, and asked Ramu to accompany her. She discussed the issue with them and was delighted to find that they were not only okay with their son marrying Saira but also happy. The three called Soumen from there. He was happily amazed to hear the details she had worked out. He had always found his *Thakurma* strong and determined, and marveled that age had hardly ebbed her enthusiasm and grit.

Soumen kept the phone down, emotional, but assured.

After spending a few days in Lucknow, Ramu and she left for Delhi.

Surprisingly, Saira was not at all perturbed. She had been witness to the immense affection her parents had for Soumen and was confident that they would eventually agree. That they could be influenced by Maulana and Mir escaped her comprehension.

Away from her house, Saira was not aware of the extent to which her parents were opposed to the relationship. And away from Patna, she was not completely conscious of the growing bitterness between the two communities and how it had begun impacting her own case.

Seeing her unwavering faith, Damyanti asked her, 'What if they fix your marriage with someone else?'

'Never, *dadi*. They will never do that without speaking to me.'

'*Beta*, maybe you don't realize that your parents are not the only people who think that they need to have a say in who you should marry. There are more than a few involved and each with vested and ugly interests. The moment the date of the wedding is announced, it will become a political issue,' Damyanti suddenly became serious. 'People will remain quiet till you remain silent. But things will become ugly the moment they see that the marriage inevitable.'

'You are worrying too much, *dadi*,' Saira walked across and sat beside Damyanti.

'You are so naïve. You do not see, *beta*, what I see. I want to see the two of you together and happy as a couple,' Damyanti paused for some time and continued, 'I won't allow anyone to rob you of your happiness.'

Damyanti stroked Saira's hair, and then quickly changed the topic. 'So, what's your plan after completing graduation?'

'I'm planning to do Masters.'

'From?'

'Delhi University,' Saira replied, a little surprised. In her view, the only available option was Delhi University.

'And after that?'

'I'm not sure, *Dadi*. Soumen wants to work abroad for at least a few years. I would like to teach in a university or work in the area of public policy. And hence, I may do a Ph.D.'

'Since you may have to look for a teaching assignment abroad, why don't you explore doing Masters from a university in the USA?'

Saira squeezed Damyanti's cheeks. 'Is my sweet *dadi* going to pay the fees? I understand getting a full scholarship is very difficult.'

Damyanti smiled and said, 'Yes, your sweet *dadi* will pay. She has saved enough and is fit enough to resume medical practice. So, don't worry.'

Saira hugged Damyanti as her eyes became moist, 'No, *dadi*. You will need money. How can I use your money for this?'

Damyanti hugged her tighter and kissed her forehead. She walked to the table and took out a piece of paper with names of six universities. She handed over the paper to Saira and asked her to apply to those universities.

Saira was surprised, 'Where did you get the names of these universities?'

'Soumen. But don't think I'm dumb. I'm one of the earlier female doctors of this country,' Damyanti replied, with deep laughter.

'So that stupid is also involved in this grand plan!' Saira blushed.

***

Damyanti returned to Patna, to a city that was witnessing heightened activity for the Ram Mandir. Ramu often brought news of minor scuffles between members of the two communities. There were all kinds of rumors floating. Muslims were told that Hindus would attack Muslim households in Ayodhya and detonate the Babri Masjid. Hindus were told that Muslims were stocking weapons and explosives in mosques to attack them. The suspicion that one had for the other changed to fear and hatred, and only grew worse with time.

In December, when Saira came home during the winter breaks, she was presented with profiles of four prospective grooms. One of them was a doctor practicing in Ranchi and related to Mir's wife. She was surprised to learn the extent to which the discussions had progressed, especially in the case of the doctor. Her parents appeared prepared to counter her arguments. They answered as if they had anticipated each argument. In many cases, she felt that they were tutored, never having heard them bring up such issues in the past. And if it became difficult for them to counter her arguments, raking up emotions was a convenient refuge. Often, the bombardment of emotions was enough to melt her. And a few instances when Saira stood firm, they brought religion to the front, often quoting something from the Quran. In such cases, it was made amply clear to her that faith was beyond debate and discussion.

Distressed, she left for Delhi in the first week of January. At the time of departure, discreetly stuffed her passport in her suitcase.

In March, Saira received a letter of acceptance from the University of California, Berkeley, for its Master of Public Policy programme with 70% relief on tuition and living. Excited, she called up Soumen and Damyanti and was delighted to note the feeling of exultation in the latter's voice. Half way into the discussion, Damyanti was into the rest of her plan.

Saira wanted to share the news with her parents and brother, but refrained from doing so.

Damyanti wanted to speak to Zafar and Rehana one more time before Saira and Soumen took their next step. She found them scared and restrained, but not as opposed as earlier. They kept ruling out any possibility of a marriage between Saira and Soumen, but not with the same conviction as before. She felt that either Saira's resolve had had some effect on them or they had been able to see through the selfish designs of Mir and Maulana. It was evident to her that the two were in a trap. She left their house feeling pity and unsure of what they would do next.

A couple of days later, her house was attacked in the night. The windowpanes were broken, the plants in the garden uprooted, and black paint thrown all over. The next day, she received a call threatening her of dire consequences if she pursued the idea of Saira and Soumen marrying each other. The word of the attack spread like wild fire. Seeing this as an opportunity for political mileage, the Bal members again rushed to her help. Cool and composed, she refused any help from them, making it clear that it was the responsibility of the government and police to provide her protection.

Zafar and Rehana did not revert to her. Damyanti waited for a month, and then lost hope. Disappointed, she made two phone calls, one to Soumen and the other to Saira. The attack, hatred, political maneuvering, and the all-pervasive fear only strengthened her resolve.

Saira needed to leave for California by the end of August to join UC Berkeley. Damyanti deposited Rs 3 lakh, equivalent to $10,000 in Saira's account.

Soumen was going to complete his Masters and had three options. He had a job offer from a large technology company and acceptances at UC Berkeley and Carnegie Mellon University for Ph.D. programmes with a job as a teaching assistant.

Saira was going through a lot of turmoil in her head. She dialed her parents on several occasions to inform them about her plans of pursuing Masters in California but disconnected the phone after one ring. She was not comfortable taking such a step without informing them. But the more she analyzed the situation, she saw imminent threat and danger. She knew in the heated environment of the Ram Mandir movement where many were trying to gain political currency, this did not remain an issue between two individuals or families. It was an issue between two communities, and for a few leaders, it could mean political life or death. She loved her parents and had always taken a lot of pride in their sense of judgement and reason, but lately, she had been a witness to their succumbing to Maulana and Mir and losing their sense of objective. In Damyanti, she had not only found a guide but a source of strength. She concluded that she needed to take drastic steps and then work towards building back her relationship with her parents.

Soumen reached Delhi in the third week of August, a week after Damyanti, his parents and siblings had arrived. Saira and he got married on the August 21 in a Delhi court in the presence of his family, friends, and Madhav. The visit also helped him decide in favor of doing a Ph.D. and not taking up a job. In order to support Saira's Masters in the USA, he had almost decided to take up a job. But Damyanti prevailed upon everyone when she said that she would fund Saira's education. The couple left for the US via London for a stopover at Soumitro's house.

Damyanti bade them farewell with tears, some out of happiness that the two were together but a lot out of sorrow. Soumen was her life and her pride. Every time he won an award, she was the happiest, happier than when her own sons and Sahana had won similar accolades. She had dreamt of a grand wedding for him. That he had to marry in a court, against the wishes of Saira's parents and in secrecy, left her sad.

Soon, a bomb dropped at Zafar's house in the form

of a letter. Saira had written a long note to her parents expressing her dismay at the turn of events and on their turning a deaf ear to her pleas. She informed them that she had left the country and assured them that she would be safe. While she profusely apologized for her action, she voiced extreme disappointment at their falling prey to the constant vitriol of Maulana and Mir. The letter did not mention anything about the place that she was going to, what she had planned to do or her marriage with Soumen. The letter came as a shock to Rehana and Zafar. They immediately rushed to Damyanti's house.

'They are intelligent adults, mature enough to take their decisions. Please keep me out of this,' Damyanti kept uttering on repeated request from Zafar for information.

While she was worried about her own safety in the inflammable environment around her, she was more concerned that the news of the marriage could take a communal turn.

Rehana fell at her feet, crying loud, 'Please tell us where she is. What will we tell the community?' She clung to her feet, not letting her go. The mother in Damyanti could not see tears and anxiety in Rehana's eyes for long. She started crying, lifted Rehana and hugged her.

'I didn't want things to turn the way they did, Rehana. I could not see my children in pain. They are innocent, looking for happiness together, nothing more. You have known Soumen. He is a nice boy. They will be happy together,' Damyanti hugged Rehana tighter and spoke between sobs.

'Where has she gone?'

'She has gone to complete her Masters at a very prestigious university, one of the best in the world.'

'But how will she pay the fees and bear the living cost?' Zafar interrupted.

'Don't worry. She has got a large scholarship and I'm going to pay the balance.'

Damyanti walked to the sofa and slowly lowered herself on the seat.

'Are they married?' Rehana asked.

Damyanti kept quiet for some time and then replied, 'Yes, they are.'

Rehana and Zafar sank in the sofa. 'What will we tell our community and our relatives? And that too in this environment,' they uttered together, worried and devastated.

Damyanti thought for some time and then said, 'Please tell them the truth. Tell them that she got accepted at a much-respected university, one in which Jai Prakash *babu* had studied, and had to leave at a short notice.'

'No one will believe that she left suddenly, without informing anyone,' Zafar spoke, thinking hard.

Damyanti spoke immediately, as if she had anticipated

this. 'Why don't you two travel to Delhi and come back after a few days. On your return, you could tell everyone that you had gone to see her off as she had to leave urgently for college admission. Once things get normal on *mandir* movement, you could break the news gradually.'

Left with no option but to accept the situation, Zafar and Rehana got up to leave. They had walked up to the main door when Damyanti called them softly and said, 'Please come back, sit for a few more minutes. I want to share a few things.' The two came back and sat on the sofa.

Damyanti was staring out of the window, as if she was trying to dig deep into long lost memories. She began speaking after some time.

'Rehana, as a kid all I wanted was to live in Dacca, amongst my friends and family. After my marriage, though Gautam wanted to move to Calcutta or Bombay, I remained firm in my decision of staying in Dacca. My family had very close ties with a Muslim family. Not only were we engaged in business together but also had always been there for each other in good and bad times.' She became quiet again as if she was trying to remember something.

'As a kid I wanted to marry a boy of that family,' she smiled and continued, 'no, I don't know if it was love. At that small age, little did I understand such feelings. But yes, I liked him. He pampered me and was always protective. I felt safe and happy with him around me. I thought my marriage to him would convert the friendship between the two families into a permanent relationship and I would not have to leave Dacca. And then, one day, I witnessed anger and angst against my father's compounder who was in love with a Muslim girl. I overheard the heated arguments and discussion. No one had to tell me after that that my marriage to the Muslim boy was impossible.' She paused and spoke. 'I had a lot of questions at that time. My innocent mind could understand the futility of the arguments put forth by the adults, but I could barely counter.'

She thought for some time and spoke, 'The arguments of the Maulana, Mir, and the members of Bal are no different than what I had heard as a child.'

She paused for a long time as Zafar and Rehana looked at her intently.

'The men who pounced ferociously on me — Maulana, Mir, or members of Bal — are no different from the several selfish, ugly, contemptuous, and disdainful men I have encountered at various stages of my life. I had to leave East Bengal after the Noakhali massacre. I lost loved ones. And some who survived were raped, converted, and permanently scarred for life. I was witness to the carnage, sheltered by an old aunt of a Muslim friend. She risked her life to save ours. There were many who, like the old aunt, wanted to speak up against the brutal attacks and stop the mayhem but were too scared to come out. Zafar, the men brandishing knives, swords, axes were like the Maulana, Mir, and the Bal. And the old aunt and the majority like her are like you and me.'

'I lost your uncle. He should have lived longer. I met so many people during the Emergency to seek help — selfish, arrogant, and devious. They were like the Maulana, Mir and the Bal.'

'Rehana, after Gautam passed away, I found solace only in the kids. If Babban had been alive, he would have been a young man now and, who knows, a great cricketer. He was a darling. The men who killed him were no different from Maulana, Mir, and the Bal.'

'I had seen Daljit speak to Prayag after the latter returned from the 1971 war. Inspired by him, he was so full of enthusiasm, motivated to serve the country. He was shot dead, a precious life lost. I saw his gradual detachment from the views he had held so dear. The men who led him down that path were no different from the Maulana, Mir, and the Bal.'

Damyanti took off her glasses and wiped her tears. Rehana came and sat beside her. 'I lost Ravi. He was such a fine boy. He was as Riyaz is to me. The people who drove him to that insane act are no different from the Maulana, Mir, and the Bal.'

Damyanti was in tears, sobbing. 'I felt helpless during each of these incidents. But if the majority, who are like you and me, had stood up against these people, things would have been different. Zafar, I have always blamed the *outsiders* all my life. When the first partition of Bengal happened in 1905, people had blamed *outsiders*. When India was getting divided and Bengal was getting divided as a result of that, I blamed the *outsiders* for inflicting Partition on us. I held them responsible and my view only strengthened due to the way Pakistani army treated innocents of then East Pakistan.'

She paused for a long time, then spoke, 'Zafar, it took me many years and a few painful experiences to understand that boundaries don't define *outsiders*.

'Rehana, I could not have let the Maulana, Mir, and the Bal defeat me one more time. I had to win this battle once before I am converted to ashes. And most importantly, I couldn't let them win when it concerned Soumen and Saira, my children.'

'Rehana, Saira will be happy with Soumen. I know that you know it. She will be happier if Zafar and you accept this. She was so sad that the three of you were not there. Let religion not be the only determining factor. Look at them, see how much is common between them and you will realize that there could not have been a better match.'

Rehana and Zafar took a flight to Delhi the next day and returned after four days. The happy news that Saira had been admitted to the same university that Jai Prakash *babu* had studied at and that she had to leave at a short notice was shared with one and all. A packet of *motichoor ladoo* was sent to the houses of the Maulana and Mir.

***

In the first week of December, several *kar sevaks* reached Ayodhya. There was a large rally of about 1,50,000 people. Several senior leaders of BJP, including Lal Krishna Advani, Murali Manohar Joshi, and Uma Bharti spoke at the rally. The restless crowd began raising slogans and things got out of control. A young man sneaked past the police cordon and climbed the mosque with a saffron flag. Seeing him on top, the crowd rushed towards the mosque with axes and hammers. The police, vastly outnumbered, watched helplessly as the crowd began breaking the structure. In a matter of hours, the mosque was razed. The violent crowd also destroyed a few other mosques in the town.

The destruction of mosques led to communal riots in various parts of the country. The riots continued in pockets for a couple of months, leading to the loss of around 2,000 lives and loot and destruction of crores of property. The worst affected areas were Bombay, Surat, Ahmedabad, and Kanpur. Patna was relatively calmer. And for the first few days, Rehana and Zafar took shelter at Damyanti's house, the old lady guarding the house and her guests like a hawk, like all those years ago in a tiny room in Noakhali.

Epilogue

In June 1993, Samina received a letter from Damyanti. It had a photograph attached with it. In the photograph, Damyanti, dressed in a thick overcoat and woolen cap, was standing with her arms around Soumen and Saira. The picture was on a snow-capped mountain, very scenic and beautiful. Samina noticed that Damyanti looked serene.

The letter was brief.

'...*Samin, I am writing to you from Switzerland. You might have recognized Soumen in the picture and guessed that the angel next to me is Saira. Isn't she extremely beautiful, Samin? Don't they make a lovely couple? I had to come here at their insistence. Saira refused to go for the trip without me.*

They were trying to buy me an expensive Swiss watch with the money Soumen has saved. He says his teaching assistantship is quite paying. And when I refused to accept the gift, the silly girl insisted I allow her to do something for me. Samin, she is planning a holiday for you and me. She says everything will be planned and we need not worry. So, my dear sister, please plan to fly to Switzerland the next

May. And in those few days, let's live all the moments that we have missed in the last fifty years.

Samin, I wanted to share a piece of news with you. I came to Switzerland via London where I was staying with Soumitro. I met Razaq and his family there. I noticed Razaq's daughter Farha and Soumitro's son Rabin spending a lot of time together. Every evening, they would come to meet me and often my old eyes caught them leaving, holding each other's hands. They looked so good together. With a little mischief and lots of expectation, I asked them if they were in love and they simply blushed.

Samin, it has always been our dream and desire that our friendship of generations moves to a relationship and binds the two families forever. I hope they get married and our families become one.

Please convey my love to all.'

Samina reread the letter many times before putting it down, her eyes too wet to focus. She would pray for it, she thought. Not that she hadn't for so much, but that had never come true. She would pray yet again.